TONYA KAPPES

A

CHARMING

VOODOO

Magical Cures Mystery Series
Book ten

D1520131

Acknowledgements

WOW! Another Magical Cures Mystery Novel! I'm beyond thrilled that the readers love this series enough for there to be eleven books and counting in the series. Thank you so much for loving June and keeping her alive by buying and reading her life and stories.

Thank you to Jessica Fischer for all and I mean ALL of her amazing cover ideas and help! Amazing!

Thank you to Cyndy Ranzau for editing and making the novel shine.

Lastly, this novel was written the weeks before the twins went off to college for their first year and my youngest to start his senior year of high school. It was a transition time for me and an unfamiliar territory. Being in Whispering Falls for those weeks were familiar and home. It brought me a lot of comfort during the transition time. Much love to my Eddy for holding down the fort while I disappeared on my vacation to Whispering Falls!

Cheers to A Charming Voodoo and many more stories to come.

Xo~Tonya

Chapter One

"Good morning." I nodded to all the tourists as I walked down the main street in Whispering Falls. I made my way past my shop, A Charming Cure, on a mission to run across the street and grab some June's Gems from Raven Mortimer. My cloak was neatly tied around my neck and flapped in the fall breeze behind me. My tall brown boots clicked with each step.

The sun had just popped over the mountain and poured its magical orange glow on the crisp fall morning. There was just something about this time of the year that got my little witchy soul all stirred up.

"Good morning, June." Gerald Regiula stood outside with a cup of coffee in his hands. His top hat sat perched on top of his head, his mustache neatly combed, and his tuxedo jacket's tails hung down to his knees. He was a dapper fellow and owner of The Gathering Grove Tea Shoppe right next to . . .

Not only did my feet stop dead in their tracks, so did my heart, but in a good way.

"I knew you'd need this once you saw that." Gerald turned to face the space that as of yesterday had been empty between his shop and Wicked Good Bakery, just where I so happened to be going. "Here you go." He stuck his gloved hand out for me to take the morning elixir.

"I. . ." I stumbled for the right words and tucked a strand of my short black bob behind my ear before I took the cup, immediately taking a sip. "I needed that."

The steam from the cup curled up around my nose and tickled my senses awake.

"Scented Swan Candle Co.," I read the name on the awning above the door that sat just beyond the ornamental gate.

All of the entrances to the shops in our little village set in the foothills of Kentucky had ornamental gates that lead up to the colorful doors of the clapboard homes that held our very own secrets and unique gifts inside them.

Whispering Falls wasn't your ordinary town. It is a magical village full of what we like to be referred to as Spiritualists. The mortal world would call us witches, but that word leaves us with a bitter taste in our mouths. It had a negative, demeaning tone to it. Gerald is a tea leaf reader so he naturally owned The Gathering Grove Tea Shoppe. I am a homeopathic healer with an amazing intuition. A Charming Cure is my shop where I sold potions or homeopathic cures for what ailed anyone who walked through my shop doors.

But it was my keen sense of intuition that told me exactly what the customer needed or what their real problem was when they walked through my shop door.

Up until a few days ago, Whispering Falls had only consisted of eleven quaint shops. The Gathering Grove and A Charming Cure were two, along with Bella's Baubles, Wicked Good Bakery, Magical Moments, A Cleansing Spirit Spa, Glorybee Pet Shop, Full Moon Treesort, Ever After Books, Mystic Lights, and Two Sisters and a Funeral as well as a police station where my husband, Oscar Park, just so happened to be a co-sheriff with Colton Lance, both wizards.

"Two in week." Gerald shook his head.

I couldn't tell if he was happy or upset about it.

"And right in time for All Hallows' Eve." I took in a deep breath, my shoulders lifted and then fell when I exhaled. "I knew I smelled a breath of fresh air on my way down the hill." I smiled.

Gerald still didn't return my smile. He was bothered.

"I don't know." He shook his head. The shadow of the top hat's bill covered his eyes. "It just seems so strange that there are two new shops in a matter of days," he said again.

"New businesses mean new tourists and new tourists are always good for business." I held the cup of coffee up in the air. "Thank you for the coffee. How are Petunia and baby Orin?"

Petunia Shrubwood was Gerald's wife and owner of Glorybee Pet Shop, which was a cover for her gift of talking to animals. They had a baby boy named Orin who was the cutest little thing.

"They are good." That brought a smile to his face. "Orin is something else." He rubbed his chin, there was pride written all over his face. "He has just started saying da-da. You are going to have to ask Petunia about it. She's beside herself because he hasn't said mama."

"You do know that da-da is much easier for a baby to say because their tongue is strong from eating and with mama, they have to be able to form their lips." I took another sip.

"You don't need to tell her that." He chuckled and waved his hand in the air. The line to his shop was starting to form out the door and it was his cue that his staff needed him.

I walked down a little bit and stopped in the front of Scented Swan Candle Co.. The awning was bright yellow with the name written in red and two red swans on each side. The gate that opened up to the path of the shop had stained glass showing long-stemmed tapered white candles with yellow flames. The sunlight hit it perfectly, making it look as though the candles were really lit.

I continued to walk next door. The heavenly smells of pastries swirled around me. My insides nearly melted into sugary goodness as soon as I opened the door.

"June," Raven Mortimer greeted me with a warm smile. Her long black hair hung in loose curls across her shoulders and down her Wicked Good apron. "How was your honeymoon?"

"Tulip Island was amazing." My eyes darted between all the delicious pastries, making it hard for me to decide which ones to pick for the now two new shop owners of Whispering Falls. "You know," I pointed behind me to the new shop that had popped up a couple days ago, "Hidden Treasure's owner, Violet Draper, actually grew up on Tulip Island and after I told her where I lived, she moved here."

"Have you been in her shop?" Raven's voice rose with excitement. "She's an amazing clothing designer. Faith has already spent her paycheck on a new wardrobe."

"Where is Faith?" I looked around.

Faith usually helped Raven out in mornings and did the morning deliveries to the surrounding mortal towns like Locust Grove, where I grew up.

"She is off snapping pictures of the new pumpkin patch for the new art gallery." Raven tossed dough in the air. She snapped her fingers and the big ball of flour exploded into an assortment of doughnuts. The ones with sprinkles caused my mouth to water. "Blue Moon Gallery."

"Blue Moon Gallery?" I hadn't seen that new shop.

"It's so cool. Since there are so many new shops, they came in this morning and asked Faith if she could do a show with her photos and do a write up in the *Gazette*." Raven opened the oven. The scent of cinnamon and sugar billowed out when she took the scones out and placed them on a white, tiered platform that sat on top of the glass counter.

"That's so cool. Where is the shop?" I asked.

"It's next to Two Sisters and a Funeral. There is all the underdeveloped land." She pointed to the right. "Have you seen the pumpkin patch?"

"No, I had no clue all of this was going up." I shook my head. "I bet Oscar is a frantic mess going around and distributing all the by-laws to them."

"He's got his hands full with all the new people." Raven smiled.

"That's why I'm here this beautiful fall morning." I dragged my finger down the glass counter and pointed to the June's Gems that were named after me and tasted exactly like my favorite treat and go-to stress relieving food, the Ding Dong. "I'll take four June's Gems, two each in two separate boxes along with a half dozen of your choice."

"That's a lot of sugar." Raven plucked two of the pink and green to-go Wicked Good Bakery boxes and started to fill them up.

"I am going to take one to Hidden Treasures and," I pointed in the direction of the new candle shop, "one to Scented Swan Candle Co. and you might as well throw in a few more for the other new businesses."

I just added them to my schedule.

"What about that? Four new shops in a couple of days." That was twice that I'd heard someone say comment on the new shops, which wouldn't normally be strange, but it sent my intuition on high alert.

"I figure they are just in time for the All Hallows' Eve celebration." The thought of our annual night before Halloween festival made me giddy.

The shops handed out candy to tourists and their children who were dressed up and pretended to be well. . .us. Last year we'd added a small carnival and I was happy to see them back again this year. It was our favorite time of the year where we could actually dress the part without being judged.

"I hope you are right." Raven did a little shimmy-shake when she handed me the boxes. My intuition went off a second time.

"I'll take a couple of June's Gems for myself." I figured I'd better get my nerves under control and June's Gems were the only thing that helped. I looked down when I felt something on my feet. "There you are," I bent down and picked up Mr. Prince Charming, my fairy-god cat.

He jumped back, not letting me pick him up.

"Meow," he purred softly as something dropped from his mouth. A sick feeling washed over me, it was the third time my intuition kicked in. Only this time, it nearly knocked me off my feet.

Chapter Two

With my mouth stuffed full of a June's Gem, the two boxes stuck under my armpit, the leaf charm Mr. Prince Charming had dropped at my feet now in my hand, and my fairy-god cat trotting next to me, I scurried across the street to Bella's Baubles.

I smacked the ornamental gate not taking in the embedded gems that made crystal rainbows on the sidewalk like I normally did. I had to see Bella. It was of the utmost importance.

The pink wooden door to the cream cottage-style shop was propped open. A few leaves shuffled across the threshold from the light fall breeze. Mr. Prince Charming batted at them.

Bella sat behind the counter with the lope held tight in her scrunched up eye. She was looking at a gem.

"I've been expecting you." She tossed her long blond hair behind her shoulder. She smiled, exposing the gap between her two front teeth. Her cheeks balled. "Our little friend brought you his present?"

"He did." I uncurled my fist and held out the leaf charm. It seemed harmless, but I knew different. "Well?" I twisted my wrist around. The already full charm bracelet jingled as she unclasped it.

"This one is about the seasonal change. It's a season of transition, it embodies a culmination. It's nature's 'last hoorah' before retiring into winter's slumbering mood. This is a hustle-bustle-boogie down month as preparations are made and he is just making sure with the new shops and development in town that you keep focused." Bella quickly added the charm to the others he'd given me.

"All of that sounds nice and flowery, but you and I both know that every charm on that bracelet came with a price. A price of protection when I needed it." I reminded her how Mr. Prince Charming was my familiar and he gave me a charm when I needed protection the most.

"Just stay true to you and listen closely to your intuition." She held the bracelet up and gestured for my wrist. A couple of tourists walked in. "Those smell divine." She tapped the boxes from Wicked Good. "Excuse me."

She got up from the chair behind the counter. She stood all of five feet, two inches, much short then me.

"Welcome to Bella's Baubles," she greeted the two women. "I've got a lovely jade pendant that will match your go-getter personality."

"How did you know I was looking for a jade stone?" the woman gasped. Her eyes popped opened as they turned to her friend.

"I told you somehow all the shops have exactly what you need." Both of them bounced on the balls of their feet in delight.

Joy filled up my troubled soul. Yes. The feeling of excitement that bubbled up in me had to do with All Hallows' Eve.

Development. My eyes lowered as I considered that Bella said something about a development.

"Excuse me," I touched Bella's arm after she showed the ladies the piece of jade. "Did you say development?"

"Yes. Isn't it wonderful?" Her eyes sparkled from the insides. "New residents and new shops. It is a special time of year."

Suddenly my intuition did it again. Something was going on that didn't sit well with me. I rubbed my hand around my wrist and felt my charms. I needed to go visit these shops and see what was going on.

"Mewl!" Mr. Prince Charming stood on his hind legs and batted the dangling charms, then he darted out the open door right before it slammed shut.

Chapter Three

The hustle and bustle on the sidewalk filled me with joy. I loved seeing all the tourists come and visit our magical village. I pulled the edges of my cape around my neck to ward off the slight fall breeze and took a deep breath of the clean autumn air letting it fill my lungs.

Slowly I exhaled and gazed above the horizon as a red-blood sun rose. The perfect weather for the All Hallows' Eve celebration. The new wooden sign at the top of the street had Whispering Falls at the top with planks of wood attached with all the different shop names pointing their way.

I looked at the new shop next to Bella's, Crazy Crafty Chick and thought it was a cute name. The cottage style shop was painted blue and had an adorable porch with a white fence around it. The wrought-iron gate had images of thread and needle, glass beads, and pottery tools.

"Good mornin'." A woman walked out of the shop and put a basket of yarn on a display table on the porch with a Grand Opening Sale sign. "I'm Leah LeRoy, a clairsentience from Alabama."

The friendly southern girl smiled. Her long brown hair was parted to the side and hung past her collarbone. She had a friendly face and sweet smile, or maybe it was the charming accent that made her so friendly. She had on a pair of jeans and simple white sweater with a monogram on the top left side.

"Hi, I'm June. . ." I walked up to the shop.

"June Heal." Her brows lifted. "I know exactly who you are." She nodded. Her blue eyes bright. "I made sure that I checked out all the shops and people before I decided to move here. My mama and daddy wouldn't have wanted me to move all the way from home if I hadn't done my homework."

"Oh," I chuckled and handed her a box of doughnuts. "Here is a welcome gift. I hope you enjoy it."

"Thank you. Every time someone opens that door and the smell crosses the street, I gain a pound." She winked. "I do hope you join me in some of my craft classes."

"I'm not so crafty," I said and pulled the cape closer to my body as the wind blew around my ankles.

Meow. Mr. Prince Charming walked over to Leah and looked up at her.

"Hi there." She bent down and patted him on the head. "You are a cutie."

He didn't pay her much attention as the basket full of yarn had captured his eye. He darted up to the porch and stood on his hind legs, sniffing the basket before he jumped up in it.

"He will drive you nuts, so just shoo him back down to my shop when he does." My eyes narrowed when I noticed him kneading the skeins before he curled up. "Mr. Prince Charming, now!"

He didn't bother lifting his head.

"I'm so sorry." I walked past Leah and walked up to get him out of the basket. "You are so naughty. People don't want cat hair all over their new yarn."

"He is adorable." Leah reached out and scratched his head. He purred.

"I hope you are participating in the All Hallows' Eve celebration." I was excited to see all the new shops and new citizens. It was going to be a wonderful celebration.

Rowl! Mr. Prince Charming smacked my bracelet before he jumped out of my arms and darted out the wrought-iron gate where he stopped and began to clean his front legs.

"Ornery cat. I better go." I waved and joined him on the sidewalk, trying to decide which shop I should go to next.

"Hey there." Oscar Park, my handsome husband walked up behind me. "You have something in there for me?" he asked when he noticed my handful of Wicked Good boxes.

"I have an extra June's Gem in my bag, but these are for all the new shops." I gave him a kiss on the lips before he dug into my black bag that was strapped across my body. "You might need two. You have a big day ahead of you."

Mr. Prince Charming stood on his hind legs and batted at my bag. He loved June's Gems and even though chocolate wasn't good for mortal cats, it was fine for my fairy-god cat. I ignored him. He trotted in front of us with his tail pointing the way.

We walked down the street toward Two Sisters and a Funeral. My plan was to take Mr. Prince Charming's lead and start at the end of town and work my way down until I needed to open my shop. Since he was my familiar and had given me the leaf charm, I figured he knew something and so I decided to follow him.

"It's very exciting to have more citizens." His blue eyes stilled. "Have you heard about Ophelia and Colton?"

"No." I looked deep into his eyes. There was something funny in them.

"They split up." He shook his head and took a big bite of the Gem.

Mr. Prince Charming ran back to us and did figure eights around my ankles and then Oscar's. He and Oscar weren't the best of friends, but he knew that I loved Oscar. It was his way of doing the infinity sign around our ankles, letting me know we are all okay.

His words wedged in my brain as I tried to process the shock.

"But they were. . ." I was too stunned to finish the sentence.

"I know." He put his arm around me and guided me down the sidewalk because my legs had stopped working. "He was sleeping on the couch in the back room of the station. I was shocked to see him there. He's a mess."

"I have to go see her." I turned, but Oscar grabbed my shoulders.

"She left town for a few days and closed her shop." There was a deep sadness in his eyes. "Colton said she was the one who ended it. That she wasn't in love with him anymore. That was it."

"Oh, gosh." I was so fond of them. They were young like us and we enjoyed doing things with them. "That hurts my heart. Maybe they will get back together."

I looked over my shoulder at Ever After Books and wondered if I could go in and do a smudge, clear out the confusion that Ophelia was obviously feeling.

"I don't like that look in your eyes," Oscar said. "You can't save them. You can't do magic on them. No love potions." He pulled out a paper from the file he was carrying. "By-laws state that you can't perform magic on or read another spiritualist."

"I know." I was well aware of the rules and well aware that when I did break one, I paid for it. "It's just so sad and shocking."

"I know." Oscar was always the voice of reason. That was one trait that made him a great cop. "We just need to be a friend to them and listen when they need a shoulder to lean on or ear to talk to."

I nodded my head.

"I do have some news." I lifted my wrist in the air and shook the bracelet.

"Oh no." Oscar stuffed the last bit of Gem in his mouth.

"It's a leaf charm." I pointed it out and continued up the sidewalk. "According to Bella it just means seasonal change. With all the new citizens and shops, I think I need to incorporate them all in the smudging, welcome them." I shrugged wanting to believe my words.

"Let's hope so." Oscar reached between us and took my hand in his. We snuggled together so the breeze couldn't get through and worked our way through the tourists to the top of the hill.

Yeah, let's hope so, my mind settled around the leaf and how change had already come as the fall wind whipped around. Ophelia and Colton's break-up sat heavy on my heart. I couldn't help but wonder if they were part of the seasonal change Bella talked about.

Chapter Four

"Mornin'!" A woman's voice trilled through the gallery and bounced off the glass walls as the bell over the door signaled our arrival. "I'm pleased to see you."

A woman with curly black hair appeared from behind a big oil painting that was hanging from the ceiling. She maneuvered her way around the canvas and wiped her hands down her white apron with cherries all over it.

"Do you like?" she asked after she stood next to us. She put her hands on her plump hips and tilted her head to the left and then to the right.

Meow, Mr. Prince Charming said as if he approved.

"I'm so glad, sir." She swooped down and bowed to him. "I'm Cherry Merry and that's my brother Perry Merry." She took a long look between Oscar and I. "You here are," she scurried up to the painting and pointed to what looked like A Charming Cure, "June Heal." Her homely face arranged itself into a smile. "And you here." She pointed to the police station across the street from my shop. "I have to confess that your uniform gave it away and I had already heard from the sisters that you two were married."

I chuckled. "For a minute I thought you had already checked us out."

"Only if you call the Karimas telling me every single bit of information checking you out, then," she threw her hands in the air, "guilty!"

Perry walked over and he shook Oscar's hand.

"We are from a village out west and were so excited to hear about the new development." She slid her eyes toward her brother. "A fresh start is always good."

"Welcome." I tried not to let my intuition go wild and tried to figure out what she meant by a fresh start.

"I'm beyond thrilled I could use my own shop designs and not conform to the cottage style on Main Street."

Blue Moon Gallery was two floors of full glass walls. The staircase in the middle was even glass. I could look down on the main street and see all of it. When I looked to the right, I could see my house on the hill and to the left the mountains. Right next door was Two Sisters and a Funeral Home which also wasn't like the shops on the main strip.

"Isn't it a great view?" Her cheeks balled as she smiled, beaming with pride.

"It is." I held out a box from Wicked Good. "I wanted to welcome you to Whispering Falls and if you ever need us, we are here for you."

"Thank you." She graciously took the box. "I'm thrilled that Faith Mortimer is going to take some fantastic photos and display them here the night of All Hallows' Eve."

"Here are the by-laws of the village and the meeting times for the village council. I'm sure Petunia Shrubwood will be by shortly to say hello." Oscar handed her a pack of papers like we had gotten when we moved to Whispering Falls a few years ago. "It might take her a couple of days to get over here since she has a young son as well as having to make her rounds to the other new shops and still run a business."

"I see." She reached out her hand and took the papers. "I'm sure we are going to love it here." She handed Perry the papers and the box of treats.

"Thank you for stopping by." Perry nodded before going back to the desk and continued doing what he'd been doing when we walked in. "I'm sure we will be seeing a lot of each other."

"I'm sure." I gathered my hands in front of me and clasped them. I turned to Oscar. "Are you ready?"

"I am." He smiled and took the first step to the door.

"Toodles," Cherry called as Oscar, Mr. Prince Charming and I walked out the door.

Halfway down the hill, I turned around. Cherry and Perry Merry were staring at us. There was a strange nervous unease that swept through my veins.

"They seemed nice." Oscar said as we stepped back up on the sidewalk and headed toward Scented Swan Candle Co.

"Mmhmm," was all I could muster up as my intuition roared deep within me.

"June," Oscar warned. "Don't be letting any strange feeling creep up. New citizens are a good thing. New shops are good for our village."

"Even new candles." I ran my hand along Swan's ornamental gate. "I love the stained-glass candle."

"I can now see our house all lit up." He smiled and held the gate open for me and Mr. Prince Charming.

Oscar was right. I loved scented things. That was one of the appeals of my shop. As soon as a customer walked in, they were greeted with smells they loved. It was part of the magic.

"Wow," was all I could say when I walked into Scented Swan. It was like I'd stepped out of Whispering Falls and into the country of Greece.

The walls were painted a muted green and the architectural details reminded me of ancient gods with its doomed features and cut-outs. Wood shelving of different sizes and shapes were built into the walls and filled with all sorts of colors and assorted sizes of candles.

There was a clay statue in the middle of the store that stood on a pillar with an ancient cement bird bath. Candles flickered with small flames as they floated around the feet of the statue in the bath. Their reflections bounced off the tile ceiling that helped circulate the scents and smells that were warm and inviting.

The walls weren't four straight walls as perceived from the outside. They were all curved and created a flow that felt good to the spirit. In the far back, near the counter where there was a line of customers, there was a row of hanging candles that had just been made as evidenced by the fresh hot wax that dripped on the floor.

"Good morning to the Park family," the chipper voice greeted us from behind the counter. "I'm Chandler Swan. Please," he gestured to the hanging candles, "take your pick."

I stepped over to get a look at them as Chandler finished up with the customers. They were all shapes and sizes. I decided on a honeycomb one that reminded me of candy corn. It would be perfect to light in the store.

"Do you have some business cards I can display in my shop?" I asked.

"I certainly do." He grabbed a few from behind his counter and handed them to me.

I put them in my bag and continued to walk around as Oscar gave Chandler the papers and went over a few rules. Chandler was a happy fellow. He wore a "go to hell" hat over his pointy nose, he was tall and thin—kinda like the skinny candles he had in the store. His five o'clock shadow was too early for a real o'clock shadow so I assumed he always wore it that way.

Faith Mortimer was in the shop snapping away with her camera and making notes on a pad of paper.

"June, isn't it fantastic?" she asked as she peered over the lens of the fancy piece of equipment. "It's such an exciting time for us."

"It is." I watched as she moved different candles together, arranging them in a perfect photo opportunity. "I'm going before the village council with my photos and asking for a real paper, not just the wind."

Faith had a wonderful spiritual gift of clairaudience. She was able to hear things in the whispers of the wind that the naked ear couldn't hear. She was also the *Whispering Falls Gazette* newspaper. If you were a subscriber, you received the newspaper in a whisper through the air, not in real paper form.

"Oh, Faith." I was happy for her. "That is fantastic news. I'll do an extra smudge." I winked and walked back to the counter where Chandler and Oscar had finished up.

"I wanted to welcome you to our village." I handed him the box from Wicked Good. "It's a wonderful time of year to open your shop. I hope you are taking part in our annual All Hallows' Eve celebration."

"I am." He cleared his throat. "Chandra Shango has already dropped off the flyers to go in my shop window."

"Good." I offered a smile and was glad to hear Chandra had taken her new position seriously.

The village council had appointed her chairperson of the All Hallows' Eve celebration which was a new position. They must've known the new shops were coming and someone needed to keep them informed.

"I'm looking forward to it," Chandler said over the ticking of the old cash register as he rang up the next person in line.

"Mr. Prince Charming," I called over to him. He was a sneaky one.

"He might hang with me for a while." Faith had him posing next to some candles as if he were doing a spread for Fancy Cats.

Oscar and I chuckled, before heading back out into the nippy fall air.

Across the street was Hidden Treasures. I'd already been to see Violet Draper since her shop opened. She and her son, Gene, had opened their shop a few days ago. Oscar and I had met Violet on our honeymoon and were so happy to see her come to Whispering Falls.

"Look." I pointed across the street to the shop that had appeared between my shop and Magical Moments. "Happy Herb."

My intuition told me I already knew who was in there.

"I'll see you later," I kissed Oscar before I scurried across the street with my eyes zeroed in on the new shop.

I couldn't contain the wide smile that curled on my face when I saw the concrete sidewalk leading up to Happy Herb was grass with stepping stones. I pushed the grass door open using the bamboo handle and stepped inside.

Rosemary, ginger, sage, lavender, and the unforgettable smell of cinnamon that I knew only KJ could bring me.

"June." The baritone voice was sweet to my ears.

"KJ!" I ran across the grassy floor of the new herb shop and threw my arms around my friend.

KJ was a Native American spiritualist from the west and when I needed ingredient refills for my potions, I whispered into the night air, letting it travel across the miles into KJ's ears. Within a day or even quicker, he'd show up at my shop with the ingredients I needed.

When I first came to Whispering Falls, his father, Kenny, had provided me with the herbs I needed. Unfortunately, Kenny had been killed, but we were blessed that KJ took his position.

"When I heard Whispering Falls was opening up the new development, I knew I had to move." He stood over six-foot-four. Normally he wore the traditional Native American clothing, but today he wore a pair of khaki pants, black shirt, but still had on the feather headdress.

"You have no idea how thrilled I am you are now living here and next to me." I clasped my hands and stood in a pleased surprise. "When I saw the sign, I knew it had to be you."

"Let me show you around." KJ's dark eyes illuminated with pride. "I have tried to keep everything separate and if you don't mind, I'd like to tell my customers to come to you if they need a specific treatment."

"Of course." I was so pleased he was there. It was going to make everything so easy with him right there.

The walls were painted with green ivy stems to go with the herb theme. There was natural wood shelving around the small shop. They were filled with packets of different herbs. He had a men's section for men's health as well as a women's section.

"I love this." I twirled the spinning floor display of the postcards of Whispering Falls.

"I wanted to have something special for the customers to tell their friends about," he said and pointed to one of the postcards with my shop on it. "We truly are a magical place and I want everyone to know."

"Me too." I stepped out of the way as a couple customers had come in. "I'll let you get back to work." I gave him a quick hug and gave him a box from Wicked Good.

"June," he stopped me before I headed out the door, "I had a vision that I gave you some Plantain even though it wasn't whispered to me."

He handed me a bundle tied with a piece of string. I curled my hand around the herb. A jolt through my veins sent an alarming skip to my lungs causing me to take a sudden breath.

Chapter Five

"Plantain?" I questioned Mr. Prince Charming as we walked up and through my gate in front of A Charming Cure. "This is not good."

Plantain was a special herb used for protection from evil spirits and snake bites, removing weariness, healing headaches, house & business blessings.

Darla always placed a pinch of dried Plantain leaves in the flame of a candle or she threw it into an east wind for healing. She also hung Plantain leaves in the car for protection from evil and jealousy.

A fierce wind came sliding down over the mountains and blew dried leaves around the village.

"Let's go," I said to my fairy-god cat and scurried up the steps and let the waiting customers in the shop.

I flipped the sign and turned on the lights. An instant calm swept over me as I took off my cape and hung it on the coat tree next to the counter. My eyes shifted up to the framed photo of my parents on the wall next to the counter. It was the only photo I had of them.

"Good morning." I greeted everyone as they walked around and picked up the different potion bottles, uncorking them as they brought them to their noses and smelled the contents.

The satisfaction on their faces told me the incredible magic that was individualized was working. Whenever they smelled one of my potions, it took on a smell that that individual enjoyed.

I walked behind the counter where my cauldron was hidden behind a partition, away from wandering eyes and flipped it on.

I smiled as the cauldron filled with a watery mixture and swirled, ready for the day's work ahead. I added the Plantain to the smudging bundles so I wouldn't forget to use it during the lighting.

The Magical Cures Book from Darla, my mother, caught my attention as it flipped open from underneath the counter. The book was full of magical potions for me, but to the naked eye it was only a book of recipes. Thank goodness because I didn't want it to get into the wrong hands.

The book flipped open to a candle lighting ceremony using a honeycomb candle and a pinch of Plantain.

Mewl, Mr. Prince Charming walked around the corner of the desk and dragged his tail along the shelf where the book was sitting.

"You know exactly what I need." I bent down and picked him up. He purred in my arms.

I continued to hold him as I retrieved the candle I'd gotten from Scented Swan. I pinched a piece of the Plantain off of the bundle KJ had given me. Before I lit it and did a quickie spell, I looked around the shop to make sure no one needed me.

Since it didn't look like a spell, and I was simply lighting a candle, I decided to do it on the counter so the flame could flicker all day. I set Mr. Prince Charming down next to the candle. He sat with his eyes on the wick.

Eckla, va, brum, de, sar, la, tom, I repeated in my head a couple of times as I lit the candle. *Protect the village with all your might, especially on the night of fright. All Hallows' Eve is a place for fun for all the spirited ones.*

The candlewick flickered as I dropped the pinch of Plantain on the wick, but completely blew out when the door opened and two new spiritualists walked in.

"That's just a coincidence." My eyes drew down to Mr. Prince Charming who pawed at my wrist. I quickly lit the flame again and took out the business cards Chandler Swan had given me to place next to the honeycomb candle.

"You must be June Heal." The young man trotted up to the counter with his hand out. I gave it to him and he pulled it to his lips, kissing it gently on the back.

"You must be Patch Potter." My eyes danced as he entertained me with his bowing, blowing, huffing and puffing as he pulled a pumpkin from the pocket of his overalls.

"This is my brother Patty Potter." He rolled his hands until they opened to display another young man standing with him. "I'm here to invite you to a special preview of the pumpkin patch tonight and give you this amazing pumpkin for your window."

"Thank you, Patch." I was happy to see another happy new citizen to our village.

Patch was a little different. He was tall and lanky with orange hair just like his pumpkin. He wore a pair of worn brown laced boots and overalls with a patch on the right knee along with a black plaid shirt underneath.

"I'm beyond thrilled to have moved to the new development." He pointed to Patty. "Patty is in town only to help me move."

"Oh, you won't stay?" I asked Patty. He offered a gentle smile and shook his head. "Not even a little bit of magic will keep you here?" I winked.

"Not in the slightest," Patch rolled his eyes. "Who wouldn't love this village?" He handed me a flyer with the location and times the pumpkin patch would be open to the public.

"Thank you for the invitation." I walked around the front of the counter and began to walk them to the door with the pumpkin in my hand. "I will definitely be there."

I waved them off and shut the door behind them. The front window display of my shop had already been transformed into an All Hallows' Eve celebration display with pumpkins, hay bales, a fodder shock and a scarecrow. I placed Patch's pumpkin at the feet of the scarecrow. I stuck his flyer on the glass of the window and slid my eyes across the street to Ever After Books.

It was dark and sad. Not like a bookstore should be.

"Hello! June?" Faith's voice brought me out of my stare and I took a deep breath.

"Over here." I walked out and offered my friend a hug. "You did wonders with the window display. I just added a pumpkin from Patch Potter." I pointed to the door. "Did you see him and his brother on the way out?"

"No." A look of sadness drew across her face. "Shame too. I heard his pumpkin patch is amazing and I can't wait until I can go see it and take pictures."

"I heard about the big gallery display." I was excited for my friend. I ran a hand down her arm and didn't feel the same excitement. "Are you okay?"

"Let me guess who told you." Her eyes narrowed. She brushed back a strand of her blond hair. "Raven."

"No, Cherry Perry told me." I couldn't help but wonder what the tone in her voice meant. "Raven seemed happy. Is she not?"

"It's nothing." She shook it off. "I just wanted to pop by and make sure you liked the display."

"I love it." I watched her give Mr. Prince Charming some love before I waved her off as she left.

I drew my eyes back over toward Ever After Books and then down the street toward Wicked Good before the smell of pumpkin circled around my head and I followed the scent to the honeycomb candle.

Chapter Six

"It's your active imagination." Oscar sat at our kitchen table finishing up the last bite of homemade cornbread and beans I'd fixed for supper.

There weren't too many nights we were home together and I generally never cooked, but beans and cornbread were one of Oscar's favorites that Darla made when we were growing up. It was one of few dishes she made that wasn't pulled straight from her garden.

"I'm telling you. Somehow Wicked Good, Ever After Books and Patch's Pumpkins are in a universal bond." I knew it was risky telling Oscar about the feelings I'd been having all day about the three shops, or maybe the three shop owners. "You know that my intuition is rarely wrong."

It was true. My intuition just so happened to be one of my spiritual gifts and if I didn't listen to it, that's when trouble happened.

"You know that candle I bought from Scented Swan?" I asked and took his plate from him. "It smelled like pumpkin."

I put the plate in the dishwasher and finished cleaning up the dishes.

"Oh, no," Oscar's voice trilled a spooky tone as he joked. "Maybe everything in Whispering Falls smells like pumpkin."

"Yeah, I guess you're right." I bit the edge of my lip trying to get the gnawing feeling from my gut. From the spiced lattes at The Gathering Grove to the pumpkin squash and buffet at Full Moon Treesort, pumpkin was floating through the air.

"When we are together tonight for the big pumpkin patch unveiling, then you will feel so much better." Oscar stood up and dragged me into his arms. There really was nothing safer than being held by him.

"Have you seen Colton?" I asked, wondering how Ophelia was doing and where she had gone. "I wonder what he did to her?"

"He did to her?" Oscar laughed sarcastically. "She's the one who left town."

"Exactly. He must've done something awful for her to do that." I sighed and looked out the kitchen window and down on the village that was now only visible through the gas lamp carriage lights that dotted the sidewalk.

"I can't help but think she did something and skipped town." Oscar's words bit my insides.

"I'm not going to argue about who did what. All I know is that he said that he needed time off and that he was going back west to visit family." Oscar's eyes saddened. "I hate this. I wish the spiritual world was free of such acts between a couple."

"Well," I squeezed him tight. "It's not going to happen to us."

"No it's not." All of my stress relieved as soon as his lips covered mine.

Rowl! Mr. Prince Charming jumped up on the counter interrupting us as someone knocked on the door.

"Perfect timing." Oscar lifted a brow at Mr. Prince Charming. He opened the door while I put the last dish in the dishwasher. "Aunt Eloise."

Oscar fully opened the door and his aunt, Eloise Sandlewood, glided into the house. She pulled off the hood of her cape and ran her fingertips through her short red, spiky hair. Her emerald eyes glittered with delight.

"I was on my way to the pumpkin patch and I saw some lights on." She hugged Oscar and then slid across the floor to embrace me. "Are you two going?"

"We were just about to leave." I hugged back before I pulled away. "Let me change my clothes and we can all go together."

"Fabulous." She drew her hands together. "How is the shop?"

"It's going great. Have you been to any of the new shops yet?" I asked from the bedroom. I walked over to Madame Torres, my crystal ball, and waved a hand over her. "You are going to love the new candle shop."

"Scented Swan? I've already been there." Her voice echoed down the hall.

The inside of Madame Torres was a calming sea of blue. Twice I tapped the top of her globe to see if there was anything I needed to know. She didn't appear, so that set my mind at ease.

Quickly I changed into a pair of jeans and a thicker sweater. When Eloise came into the house, I felt the wind whip right on in.

"Are you ready?" I asked the two of them after I was finished.

Everyone, even Mr. Prince Charming nodded.

"Walk or ride?" I pointed to The Green Machine, what I loving called my green El Camino.

"It's such a lovely night." The full moon shone bright overhead. "Why don't we walk?"

"There isn't anything I'd like more than to be with my favorite women." Oscar got in between me and Eloise and put his arms around our shoulders.

Eloise and I laughed.

"Did you see KJ today?" She looked around Oscar as we walked down the hill toward the village.

Potter's Pumpkin Patch was in the area behind the police station. Mr. Prince Charming led the way through the night as his white tail glowed and waved in the air ahead. The fireflies played tag with one another as they made a straight path for us to walk.

"I was so shocked when I saw Happy Herb. I instantly knew it was him." There was such a sense of relief to know that he'd come to live in Whispering Falls.

"With all the new shops, I'm going to have to start extra early in the mornings." Even though she already got up before the first rooster crowed, Eloise loved and took her job very seriously as she cleansed our village every morning in her incense ritual.

I loved being with her. She and Darla had been best friends when my father was alive and we lived in Whispering Falls. Since Darla wasn't a spiritualist and my father had married a mortal, Darla couldn't live here any longer and that's when she moved me to Locust Grove and where I met Oscar. Who. . .long story short, was also a spiritualist raised by a mortal uncle. Another story, another time. What mattered now was the here and now and that Oscar and I were now happily married.

"I'm sorry to hear about your friends Ophelia Biblio and Colton Lance." Eloise paused and continued in a silky tone, "Sometimes things do not work out and it's best to find out young."

Oscar and I didn't say anything. Colton was his friend and Ophelia was mine. It was natural to take opposite sides.

The village street was nice and quiet. Arabella Paxton, florist and owner of Magical Moments, always did a beautiful job on the hanging baskets from the carriage light posts. This year she'd hung carved pumpkins with bright yellow and red mums coming out of the top. Instead of the pumpkins having the traditional faces, some had

Whispering Falls carved out while others had *All Hallows' Eve* etched into it.

As soon as we walked past the police station, we could see a big bonfire off in the distance.

"Need a ride?" Petunia Shrubwood pulled up next to us. She was in a wagon pulled by two horses. The wagon was filled with hay and a few of the new citizens from the new development.

"We'd love one." My insides jumped with giddiness.

Oscar helped Eloise and I up. We found an empty bale to sit on with a couple of blankets folded up just for our laps. Mr. Prince Charming sat in the riding seat with Petunia. I smiled when I saw them talking to each other. He loved Petunia. She understood him because of her spiritual gift as an animal reader.

"Where is Baby Orin tonight?" I asked when I noticed he wasn't attached to her like he normally was.

"He's home with Gerald. Way past his bedtime." She shoo'ed the fireflies away from the horses as they teased them. "Teenagers," she grumbled and flung the reins for the horses to move.

The fireflies darted off into the night. They were the teenagers of the spiritual world. Like most teens, they stayed up all night bugging the heck out of anyone that would be bothered with them and slept all day.

There was so much going on at Patch's. There was a stand for caramel apples, apple cider in a big cauldron, and hayrides into the field filled with the biggest and heartiest pumpkins I'd ever seen. They were still attached to the vines that came up out of the ground and curled around.

After we got off the wagon, I decided to walk around and take it all in. All of my old friends and new friends were gathered around, smiling and having community time.

Mr. Prince Charming walked next to me with his tail swaying in the nighttime air.

I walked along the vines and was amazed at how they curled and ended at the stem of the big pumpkins.

"Look, Mommy!" A little girl with her brown hair braided in pigtails ran over to Mr. Prince Charming. "A cat!"

Mr. Prince Charming looked like a show pony prancing around the little girl. I swear if I didn't know better, the darn cat was grinning ear-to-ear. He dragged his tail along the little girl's legs making her giggle.

He looked at me and I shook my head before he went back to making her laugh.

"I'm so sorry." The mom came up and took the little girl by the hand. "She's been dying to get a cat since we moved here."

"She's fine. He loves children." I tilted my head to get a good look at the mom. Her hair was cut in the cutest pixie haircut. "Have you been to Glorybee Pet Shop?"

"We have and Jo Ellen wants every animal in there." She laughed and patted her daughter on the head. "Isn't that right?"

By this time, Mr. Prince Charming had jumped up on top of the big pumpkin and walked in circles as his tail dragged back and forth under Jo Ellen's nose, making her laugh even more.

"I want this one." Jo Ellen picked up Mr. Prince Charming.

He didn't seem to mind dangling from the grip she had around his waist.

"Honey, this nice lady." The mom searched my face.

"June. June Heal." I couldn't help but try to read the mom and see what her spiritual gift was, but my intuition told me nothing. Which was very odd. The first thing I had done when I realized I was a witch was go to Hidden Halls, A Spiritualist University and attend intuition classes. "I own A Charming Cure right down from Glorybee."

"This is Ms. Heal and that's *her* cat," the mom said.

"June. You can call me June." My heart nearly stopped.

I sounded just like Darla. My mom had never liked to be call Mrs., Ms., Miss, or even Mom.

"June, can I come to your store and play with him?" Jo Ellen asked.

"Anytime." My gut tugged at the little girl's smile and joy that was in her eyes.

I gulped. Oscar and I had never talked about having our own children and I'd never planned on it, but there was just something so endearing seeing the little girl play with Mr. Prince Charming.

"Hi," Oscar walked up and put his arm around me. "I see Mr. Prince Charming has made a friend."

"Mr. Prince Charming?" the mom asked and chuckled. "He's definitely living up to his name because Jo is in love. I'm Tish Chapman. We moved into the new subdivision."

"The development." I nodded. "I haven't been over there yet."

"Oh, you must come visit. It's amazing." Tish lifted her brows. "I knew, as a single mom, that I wanted Jo Ellen to not only live in a beautiful neighborhood with other children, but also eat healthy."

"Eat healthy?" Oscar asked.

"I'm sorry, this is my husband and police officer Oscar Park." They shook hands. "What did you say about eating healthy?"

I wasn't following what she was saying.

"There is a twenty-five acre farm that is in the middle of the subdivision. We have a little market where we can get all the fresh fruit and vegetables we need." There was excitement all over her face.

"You work on a farm?" I asked.

"Oh, no." She shook her head. "I work in Locust Grove and that's where Jo Ellen goes to school. But there is a farmer and entire crew who work the farm and we shop there. Jo Ellen can go and help out in the chicken coop or even pick fresh berries, but we pay for the food."

"So it's sort of like the farm-to-market movement we are seeing all over the United States?" Oscar asked.

"It is and we are loving it so far." Tish looked down at Jo Ellen who still had Mr. Prince Charming dangling. "You are going to squish him. Put him back on the pumpkin."

Jo Ellen was sweet and did what her mom told her to do and darted off in the direction of the candy apple stand.

"It really has been life changing for us. Please come by for a visit and I'll show you around." Tish pointed toward her daughter and waved 'bye.

"How on Earth did we not know about this?" I asked.

"From what I gathered," Oscar wrapped his arm around me. It felt so nice. I always felt safe with him. "Locust Grove owns the land around Whispering Falls and the developer got the two-hundred acre land beyond our border approved for this sort of land development. Now, they've expanded into Whispering Falls."

"The council let them?" I asked.

"According to Petunia, the Order of Elders, while we were gone on our honeymoon, approved Whispering Falls to be opened up to mortals. That's why all the new shops are popping up, so we can still have our magical village but the mortals won't know." Oscar waved to someone in the distance. "I went over there today. So half of the land is in Locust Grove and half in Whispering Falls. Since I work for both police departments, it works out that I'll mainly stay around here more and police the new neighborhood."

"This means more business." I couldn't help but think of all the fun I was going to have working with new clients. I couldn't help but watch Jo Ellen take a big bite out of the candy apple and watch the juices dribble down her chin.

"It's a win for everyone. We can even go to their farmer's market and get fresh vegetables." Oscar ran his hand down my back. "What are you looking at?"

"Jo Ellen." I smiled. "She's the cutest little girl."

Oscar bent down and kissed me. "You are the cutest girl."

"I'm serious." I teased and pushed him on his chest. "We have never really talked about children."

"It's not like they are off the table for us." Oscar pulled me close and used his finger to tilt my chin up to greet his blue eyes. "I want a little girl who looks and acts just like you."

"I want a little boy who looks and acts like you." I winked.

"We should really practice before we really make the decision so we get it right." Oscar teased.

"You are something else, Oscar Park." I curled up on my toes and kissed him harder.

"I love you," he whispered.

"This is really something." I pulled away and let him cradle me from behind as we looked out over the pumpkin patch. "Whispering Falls has really come a long way in the past couple of years."

I did love the small magical town but knew that it wouldn't stay that way forever. Having all the new mortals living among us was going to be strange, but deep in my gut I knew it was going to be wonderful.

"Do you think there is any hope for Ophelia and Colton?" I asked, my heart heavy with sadness for our two friends.

"I don't know." Oscar let out a heavy sigh. He dropped his arms and waved toward another person I didn't know.

"Who are all these people waving to you?" I asked.

"People from the new neighborhood. I passed out my card and introduced myself when I was there today." He waved to an elderly woman as she walked by.

She decided to stop.

"Is this your little missy?" the woman asked. She had tight curls to her head, stood five feet tall and a little hunched over.

"This is June, my wife," he introduced me. "June, this is Hazel Jones."

"Nice to meet you Mrs. Jones." I held my hand out.

"Ms.," she corrected me. "I've already been down this road." She gestured between me and Oscar. "I'm a widower and I don't want no man. I'm tired of dealing with it."

"Oh. How do you like the new subdivision?" I asked.

"The agri-hood?" She giggled.

"Agri-hood?" I couldn't help but laugh at the eccentric little old woman.

"That's what we call it." She winked and took a swig from a container she was carrying. "You want a sip?" She held it out. "I make the best iced tea you've ever tasted."

"She does." Oscar nodded. "Hazel offered me some when I came by today."

"No thank you." I waved the tea off.

"You promise me you'll stop by." She pointed behind the pumpkin farm, "I live right over there with the prettiest flower garden you ever saw."

"I will stop by." I knew I had no choice but to go see this new housing development they had named the agrihood.

"I'm gonna have to fight that candy apple line." She glowered.

"I bet I can get you in there." Oscar held his elbow out to let Hazel take and she did. "June, I'll see you in a minute."

I watched as Oscar took her over to the line and got a candy apple from Raven Mortimer. Faith was taking pictures as Hazel took her first bite out of the apple. She held the apple up with the bite side showing and smiled for the camera.

Mr. Prince Charming decided to use the pumpkins as stepping stones and I knew he'd led me to the perfect one Oscar and I could carve for our cottage.

He jumped and sniffed and batted before he finally jumped on one next to the small shed.

"That's a big one." I looked down. He looked at me and batted the big orange thing with his paw.

I bent down and took a good look at it. There was no way I was going to be able to carry that thing out of here. Angry voices caught my attention. I continued to crouch next to the pumpkin. I had a habit of being nosy and overhearing conversations.

With my ear to my shoulder, I looked around the big pumpkin. Patch and Patty were standing in the shed. It was hard to tell them apart.

"No. You are not staying here." One spit his words out at his brother. "You have to go home. I had no idea this was going to happen. But now that we know, it's best you go."

"I'm not leaving," the other demanded.

"This is my pumpkin patch. You are only here to help. You're not staying," I assumed it was Patch Potter who was talking. I ducked behind the big pumpkin as he walked to the door of the shed and his eyes grazed the community that'd gathered for him. "I've found a home here. You are not welcome."

"I'm not leaving," Patty said again. "I'm staying."

"Over my dead body," Patch laughed.

"Even over your dead body." Patty didn't laugh. He stalked out of the shed and Patch cursed under his breath before he took his cell phone out of his pants pocket and made a call.

Not that I wanted to eavesdrop, but I did. I was fascinated with sibling arguments. I didn't have a sibling and never had the chance to argue with one.

"I think Patty is going to give me a problem and you need to figure out how to get rid of him." Patch told whoever it was on the other end of the phone.

"Listening in?" Aunt Helena appeared out of nowhere. Her long black cloak and pointy hat blended in with the darkness of the night, but her red boots were like a beacon.

"Shh." I put my finger up to my lips, but she wasn't about to let me.

"June Heal." She dragged me up by my arm. "You are an adult. Stop acting like a child."

"Oh, you ruin all the fun." I gave her a big hug. "I can't wait to tell you all about the you-know-what."

I wiggled my fingers in front of her face. Just recently she'd given me a temporary magical power I could use on my honeymoon. I could summon things with my fingers and have it at my disposal. She'd given it to me on a loan since we were not in the safety of Whispering Falls and had actually gone to Tulip Island, a secluded island in the Caribbean.

A witch can never be too safe.

"I heard it came in handy." She drummed her fingers together. "I see all the new mortals have arrived."

"Yeah, that's strange." Hazel still had Oscar by the arm. Old women loved him. "Did you go to the council meeting?"

"I did. The Elders approved it before we could protest, and Petunia had to take to the bed." She shrugged. "Progress is what they called it." Aunt Helena hugged me.

With a flash, she was gone.

I stood up and turned my attention back to the brothers and watched as they both went their separate ways and couldn't help but wonder what was going on or who Patch had called.

I shrugged it off because Aunt Helena was right. It wasn't my business.

Mr. Prince Charming darted over to the horses and I followed to see what he was up to.

Petunia had parked them near the wooded area that had a clear path to Full Moon Treesort. Full Moon was unlike any hotel or resort. It was a fully run, five-star accommodation, only the rooms were all located in different trees.

Mr. Prince Charming darted down the path.

"Where are you going?" I called after him and looked over my shoulder at the pumpkin patch before I headed down the path to follow him. "Mr. Prince Charming?" I called out.

In the distance I saw his tail flick before it darted to the right. As quickly as I could, I followed him.

"I told you not to come here," I heard someone whisper through the breeze.

I stopped. The hushed whispers bounced off the bare limbs and the conversation carried as an eerie wisp.

"This is where you ended up? In a town like this?" A male voice held anger. "You are better than this wimpy town where everything is all rosy."

"You have no idea, Pat. I wanted to turn my life around." When I heard Ophelia's voice, my ears stood on end. "I loved you so much, but you didn't care."

"Now that is all over. You have done the right thing by breaking up with that loser, Colton Lance." The familiar voice of Patty Potter breezed along with the soft cries of Ophelia.

"I love him. You have no idea." She sobbed. "But when he saw you and Patch yesterday, he couldn't let it go."

My heart sank. Was Oscar right? Did Ophelia leave Colton for another man? Patty Potter?

"Now you can come home. Be the true spiritualist you were meant to be. Not all of this. This is not you. You are magnificent. He kept you from that." Patty was making a case for himself.

Come home? I recalled Patch telling me earlier that they were from a spiritualist community out west and I knew Ophelia and Colton were from Ohio. At least that's what they'd told me when the moved to Whispering Falls.

Mr. Prince Charming's eyes glowed when he looked at me. My wrist warmed. I felt my bracelet.

Bella was right. The seasons were changing right along with hearts. This was not going to happen.

"Come home with me. We can start our new life," Patty replied sharply.

"If you think I'm going back there with you, you have another thing coming." Ophelia's laugh raked her. A shuffle of leaves were followed up by Ophelia, "Stop it. You are hurting me."

"I won't let you stay here," Patty's voice held anger. "I lost you once. Now I have found you."

"Mr. Prince Charming!" I called out. "Where are you?" I shuffled my way through the woods until I stumbled upon them. "Ophelia?"

"June." Ophelia jerked away from Patty's grip.

"Patty Potter." I nodded, my eyes hooded. "I see you met our amazing bibliophile and true to her name, Ophelia Biblio."

He didn't respond.

I jerked my head side-to-side and looked around on the ground.

"You haven't seen that cat of mine have you?" I asked, glancing between the two of them.

"No, June." Ophelia wouldn't look at me. "I'm going back to the shop now."

Ophelia took a step toward the path.

"Wait and I'll go with you." I scurried alongside her, but not without giving the *you better back off* look to Patty. "He can't leave Whispering Falls soon enough. I got an eerie feeling about him when he came into my shop today."

"Did he ask you any questions about me?" Ophelia asked.

"No, why? Do you know him?" I questioned, trying to give her a chance to explain what I'd heard and seen back there.

"No," her voice was soft. Her face was only a black outline in the darkness. I longed to see the mass of curly honey hair as the shadow of the empty tree branches parted and the moonbeam shone down on us as she made it to the back side of Glorybee Pet Shop.

"You can't possibly know him since he's from a western community and you are from a Midwestern community." I had to get to the bottom of exactly how they knew each other without going against the by-laws and reading her.

Instead of the sweet face of my friend, it was a tear-stained, confused face. Her lips remained closed. I could tell I wasn't going to get anywhere with her tonight; maybe a good night's sleep would do her good.

"Are you okay?" I asked. "You know I'm here for you."

"I know." She shook from her toes to her head. "I think it's best I just go back to Ever After and get some things so I can go clear my head."

"Get some things?" I asked.

"Yes. I think I need a mini-vacation." She sucked in a deep breath.

"Please, let me help you." I literally begged from the bottom steps of the shop. "I have a house in Locust Grove. No one will bother you there."

"No. I can't." She ran up to the door and paused to look back at me. "June," her voice turned sharp, "we are a dying breed." With that she turned and disappeared inside.

Mr. Prince Charming and I stood there for a minute, hoping she'd come back outside.

"Not a good night at the pumpkin patch?" Gerald called from across the street. He was standing between A Charming Cure and A Cleansing Spirit Spa in front of the singing Nettles with Baby Orin tucked in a carrier around his middle.

"It's fine." Mr. Prince Charming and I crossed the street and walked along the sidewalk as did he and we met in the middle in front of Glorybee Pet Shop. "Not a good night for Orin?" I asked and ran my hand down his back.

He was such a cute baby and a joy to our village. He watched as kittens jumped and played in the display window of the pet shop.

"He has a case of the croup." Gerald bounced up and down. "The night air and the singing Nettles help calm him down."

"And the kittens." I smiled at the sight of Orin as he giggled in delight as one of the kittens pawed the window as if it knew to entertain Orin. "They are so cute."

"Someone just dumped them at the back door of the shop," Gerald said. "You know Petunia." He shook his head.

"Really?" I wondered who could do such a thing. We weren't used to that in Whispering Falls.

"They are adorable," he noted. "Hopefully with the new citizens coming in, she won't have a problem adopting them out."

"Very true." I put my palm up on the window and Jo Ellen's sweet face popped in my head.

All the kittens had lined up like little soldiers and stared as Mr. Prince Charming sat at my feet and looked up at them. His tail swished back and forth sweeping the ground. "I know where I'm going to find you later," I joked because I always knew if Mr. Prince Charming wasn't around, he was probably with Petunia at Glorybee. "That one looks like you," I said to Mr. Prince Charming and pointed to the tiny white kitten.

"She's the runt." Gerald rubbed his hand down Orin's back and bounced at the same time. My heart warmed seeing Gerald so affectionate. He could be a bit brash.

"I just might have someone in mind for her." I smiled and sent out a simple wish into the cool breeze as it swept past my nose. "Aww," I whispered. "Orin is asleep."

"I must go." Gerald scurried. "I have to take advantage of sleep myself when he is slumbering."

I waved him off and ran between the police station and Ever After books to go back to the pumpkin patch and give Patty Potter a piece of my mind.

But I was too late. There was a crowd gathered in a circle around the middle of the pumpkin patch where Colton Lance and one of the Potters were in an all-out fist fight.

"I told you never to show up here or I was going to kill you!" Colton's arm lifted and came crashing down on Patty's or Patch's face—I didn't know who for sure as it was so hard to tell them apart.

The Potter twin knocked Colton with the butt of his hand, sending Colton midair. Blood dripping from both men's lips.

Faith was taking pictures of the fight and writing notes.

"Stop taking my picture!" the Potter screamed at her.

"Smile." Faith laughed and took another one just as he pointed at her. "This is going to make the front page of the *Whispering Falls Gazette*."

"Patty!" Patch pushed his way through the crowd. "Stop this now!"

Ophelia had a tiff with Patty and now Colton? My eyes narrowed as my gut signaled a war waging between the two families. The grey clouds that clashed with the starry black universe blotted out the perfect fall night sky, putting a shadow over the festivities.

"If you print that or any of those other pictures, you will regret you ever saw me!" Patty yelled at Faith before Oscar ran in between the two men and put his hands between them to stop the fight.

Faith snarled.

"What other pictures?" I asked her, trying to take her aside and out of the way.

"I came by last night to get some shots while the full moon was out. It made a beautiful scape that I knew I could put in the new gallery. At first I thought he was Patch because they look so much alike, but when he told me it wasn't open and I was trespassing, he kinda went berserk." She pushed back her blond hair and watched as Oscar tried to calm the two men down.

"Berserk how?" My face contorted.

"He demand that I hand over my camera and I told him no. He said that I couldn't print the photos and I didn't have permission. He even tried to reach for it, but I took off. He spit out some sort of idle threats but I didn't bother turning around to listen to him." She shrugged. "I was going to tell Patch about it tonight but it seems he has his hands full."

We looked over at Patch as he whispered something in Patty's ear while Oscar dispersed the crowd but kept Colton next to him for safe keeping. Patch led Patty back to his house in the new development, signaling the rest of the celebration was over. Even the teenagers went home, not sticking around to light our way back up the hill as Oscar, Mr. Prince Charming and I headed home.

Both of us were too tired to even talk about what had happened. Oscar just said that he'd feared when he heard the new development, which meant more citizens, had come to the village, the crime rate would go up like every other place in our great land.

We both tossed and turned fitfully and just as it seemed like we were both asleep, the fiery glow of Madame Torres woke me up. It wasn't like I was in a deep sleep because after last night's events at the pumpkin patch, it was hard to even fall asleep.

"Juuunnne," Madame Torres's voice rose with the red waves that curled deep inside her ball. "You must wake. You must seek. You must defend."

I rolled over and looked at my crystal ball through sleepy eyes. Mr. Prince Charming sat next to her and batted the charm bracelet I'd taken off before bed.

"Juuuunnnneeee," Madame Torres just sounded plain creepy. I sat up in bed, pushed my bangs back and looked at her. "You must wake. You must seek. You must defend."

"What does that mean?" I asked, rousing Oscar out of his slumber.

He sat up.

"What's going on?" he asked. "It's four in the morning," he said in his sleepy voice. He lifted his arms in the air, stretched and yawned.

The faint sound of an ambulance drifted up the hill and into our cottage. Oscar and I looked at each other.

"Karimas," both of us said in unison, knowing exactly what that meant.

We jumped out of bed and quickly got our clothes on.

"Where are the sisters going?" I asked Madame Torres. The red sea in her glass formed a red pumpkin with a voodoo doll etched in it. "Patch," I gulped hoping the newest member of our village hadn't already met his untimely death.

Oscar and I made it in record time to where the Karimas had driven right through the pumpkin patch, not leaving one poor pumpkin intact. The moon had been covered by dark clouds, leaving the Karimas to use their other senses.

"I smell it, sister." Constance Karima had her nose lifted in the air sniffing.

"I smell it too, sister," Patience Karima repeated her twin.

Oscar and I sat back and let them do their thing. They were the owners of Two Sisters and a Funeral. They were ghost whisperers and could smell death. Sometimes before it even came, which I had hoped was the case this time.

Their noses jiggled up and down underneath the wire-rimmed glasses perched on their noses. Their black thick-soled shoes shuffled through the thick vines as they stepped over the pumpkins the tires of their ambulance had spared. The only sound was the rustle of their house dresses with each step they took.

I started to follow them quietly before I broke the silence screaming as I fell to the ground just as the clouds parted from the big full moon and I noticed I was face-to-face with a very dead man.

Patch Potter hadn't met his untimely demise. Patty Potter had, the dried blood on his lip told me it was him.

Chapter Seven

"I told you I smelled something." Constance Karima scratched the depths of her curly grey hair and looked down at the large orange pumpkin with a dead Patty draped over it. "It's a rotten something and I don't mean the pumpkin either."

"Sister is good at pickin' out the bad dead from the good dead." Patience rubbed her hands together.

"We sure do love a fresh one." Constance rubbed her hands together and licked her lips.

"Fresh one," Patience mimicked Constance.

The twins lifted their heads. Their green eyes sparkled with delight at the sight in front of them.

"And I wonder who got him," Constance's eyes grazed the citizens that'd gathered since we'd arrived.

"Do you know how he died?" I asked and watched as Oscar and the sisters inspected the body.

"It's hard telling. But I do know it was a homicide." Constance wiggled her eyes. "My favorite kind of autopsy because they are like puzzles."

"Sister and I love puzzles." Patience bent down and pointed to something sticking out of his side. "Lookie here."

Oscar bent down. He tilted his head side-to-side and inspected what Patience had pointed to. He halted as though he was in shock. He stood back, turning to the crowd as if he were specifically looking for something or someone.

"Can you go get a sheet and the church cart?" Oscar asked the sisters. His voice held an edge that I hadn't heard in a very long time. At least not since he'd found out that his uncle Jordan was the one who had killed his parents.

The sisters didn't say anything or ask any questions. They did what Oscar had asked them to do.

"Are you okay?" I asked, even though I knew he wasn't.

"I'm afraid he's been murdered. And whoever did it used him as a pin cushion." Oscar's voice drifted into a hushed whisper. There was fear deep in his blue eyes.

"What?" I looked down at Patty and noticed he was stuck in the side with several wands.

I gulped remembering the fight he and Colton just had.

The wheels on the church cart squealed as the Karima sisters pushed it through the pumpkin patch. They proceeded to pick him up and place him on the cart under a sheet.

"Umm. . ." Patience drew her hands up to her mouth. She gasped, panting in terror before she had to look away.

"Oscar." Constance pointed to the pumpkin Patty's body had been draped over. Not only did the pumpkin have needles stuck in all over it, there was a doll that seemed to have the same markings on its body as Patty had.

A voodoo doll.

Oscar sucked in a deep breath. His eyes slid up to mine. A wave of panic rioted within me. We hadn't seen anything like this in Whispering Falls since before we let the Dark-Siders join the community.

Ahem, Gerald Regiula walked up and cleared his throat. In a loud voice, he stated, "I want everyone to know that I was against the new development and the new shops."

"Not now, Gerald." Oscar put the palm of his hand up to Gerald's chest to stop him from continuing on. "You can state your concerns at the village meeting tonight."

The sisters rolled the cart along the vines and Patty's body bopped and hopped right along with them. I tried to take my eyes off of the wands that were sticking out from underneath the sheet because I knew there were only two people who carried wands, Oscar and Colton. Oscar had been with me all night and had no reason to kill Patty, but Colton was another story. He had a wand and a very public fight with Patty. Though I couldn't forget Patty was found dead in his brother's pumpkin patch where they'd also had a very big fight. If I recalled correctly, I'd overhead Patch say *over my dead body*.

I gulped.

The sisters hit a bigger bump, sending Patty's hand flying out from underneath the sheet.

My eyes popped open as they focused on the dried chocolate and cream filling on his fingers. I flinched and struggled with the uncertainty that'd risen deep in my gut.

Colton and Patch were definitely the obvious choices on who could have played a hand in Patty's death. But. . .I glanced over the crowd and stopped when my eyes met Faith Mortimer's.

She stared back at me. Her eyes closed, as if she were guarding a secret.

Chapter Eight

Hear ye, hear ye! This is a special announcement from your Village President Petunia Shrubwood: It's unfortunate that Patty Potter has died such an untimely death while visiting his brother, Patch Potter. It's an isolated incident and there is no need to panic. The Whispering Falls Police Department has everything under control and our village is very safe.

We have decided to move our council meeting to lunchtime. For all the new citizens, our council meetings take place at The Gathering Rock that sits up on the hill behind A Charming Cure. Please be there around noon as June Heal will be holding a smudge ceremony to start us off.

On the agenda, we will be discussing All Hallows' Eve, the new development, as well as introducing the owners of the new shops. After the meeting, Amethyst Plum, proprietor of Full Moon Treesort will be hosting a reception for all the new citizens of Whispering Falls. Please join us for food and spirits.

Also in today's news, Faith's voice whispered into the air the remaining news items. Finally ending with, *today's* Whispering Falls Gazette *is brought to you by Patch's Pumpkins. Come visit today and pick out the perfect pumpkin for your All Hallows' Eve celebration. Enjoy a hayride with your family and stop at the caramel apple stand.*

The shock of finding Patty had worn off by the time Oscar had finished investigating the scene. He'd bagged the voodoo doll so he could run some prints on it and see if there were any other clues or fibers. He'd also told the

Karima sisters to put a rush on the autopsy and make sure not to touch any of the wands.

"This isn't good." Oscar shook his head on our way back up to the cottage. "I'm going to change into my uniform and make a quick call to Colton before I head out to see Patch."

"I'm going with you." I glanced over my shoulder and looked down the hill back over Whispering Falls.

Strange and haunting leaves blew through the street and curled around Eloise. She eased down the street swinging the incense back and forth in the light of the breaking sunrise. Her mouth opened and closed as she chanted good intentions over the billowing smoke. She stopped in front of A Charming Cure and did an extra swing. The chains clinked on the way down next to her leg as she swooped it back into the air.

Mr. Prince Charming darted in front of us.

"June, I don't think you need to get involved." Oscar never wanted to put me in danger.

"You and I both know that you are going to need an extra set of hands since," I gulped, "Colton. . ." I couldn't stand to finish the sentence.

"I wonder why he was so angry at Patty?" Oscar unlocked our door and we walked in to get the keys to the Green Machine. I waited while Oscar headed to the bedroom to change into his uniform.

"Well." I bit my lip. As much as I didn't want to give Colton a motive, I knew I had to tell Oscar. As he got ready, I told him what I had done while everyone was enjoying the pumpkin patch. "Last night when we were at the pumpkin patch, I decided to walk around while everyone was having a good time and. . ." My mouth dropped.

"What?" Oscar asked. He grabbed the keys off the counter and stood at the door.

"We need to go see Patch." I scurried past him and out the door. Mr. Prince Charming ran next to me.

"June, you aren't going." Oscar planted himself in between me and the car.

"Listen, I think there are more people than just Colton who had a reason to kill Patty." I put my hands on my hips and tilted my head. "And if you want to know who, then you are going to have to include me because these people are my friends too."

Oscar searched my face as if he was reaching into my thoughts.

He stepped to the side and I sat down in the driver's seat. Mr. Prince Charming jumped in and climbed up on the dashboard while Oscar got into the passenger side.

"Tell me what you know." Oscar draped his arm over the back of the seat as I drove the Green Machine down the hill and toward the new development.

I told him about how I overheard Patch and Patty arguing. Patch told Patty he couldn't stay and that's when his comment *over my dead body* came into play—only it had to be over Patty's dead body.

"Then," I gripped the wheel, "Mr. Prince Charming darted off toward Full Moon Treesort."

"Let me guess, you followed him?" Oscar dropped his eyes and looked at me with a steady gaze.

"Of course. And he wanted me to." I held the wheel steady with one hand and reached up to drag my hand down my fairy-god cat who was nestled near the windshield. "He led me straight to Patty who was being very aggressive with Ophelia Biblio."

"Huh? What?" Oscar stammered in bewilderment.

"Yes. She told him he had to leave and he told her he wasn't going anywhere without her. It was awful, so I pretended to be looking for Mr. Prince Charming." I sucked in a deep breath. Mr. Prince Charming looked up when I said his name, but quickly put it back down. "I walked her back to the bookstore. She told me she didn't want to talk about it. But he'd grabbed her." My voice cracked, "But how do they know each other? The Potters are from the west and Ophelia is from Ohio."

"Maybe they crossed paths somewhere? She could've been the one who killed him. I will need to stop by and ask her about the fight." Oscar's words haunted me. "If she and Colton are on the outs, then maybe she framed him."

"Maybe, but she loves Colton." I said in a hushed whisper, hoping that Ophelia would never do anything like that. And if she did, what would be a good reason? "But that's not all."

"There's more?" Oscar asked in a grudging voice.

"Patty and Faith Mortimer also got into it. She was taking all sorts of photos the night before and Patty demanded to see her camera and stop taking photos. She refused to let him and he told her that she couldn't print any of the ones she'd taken. Now, she'd taken pictures of the fight and he argued with her then too." I could see the new development ahead of me.

"That gives us four people to question." The look on Oscar's face scared me. "Three of the people we are friends with."

"I know." I sucked in a deep breath. Mr. Prince Charming raised his head and looked at me. I loved how he was so in tune with me. He was a good fairy-god cat.

The new development wasn't nearly what I thought it was going to look like. All the houses were different and unique.

"This is different." I turned the Green Machine into the entrance.

"It's pretty neat actually." Oscar pointed me where to turn. "Right over there is the farm where they grow the crops and straight back there is the market they've set up for the neighbors to shop. I like the fact that we can purchase from them too."

It was a pretty neat concept of whole living. I loved the idea that it was open to our village and I could take advantage of the fresh produce.

"Darla would've loved this." I sighed knowing how much Darla appreciated fresh foods. Oscar reached over and rubbed my hand. He knew it was still hard for me that I didn't have my parents. Especially Darla since I'd been raised by her.

"She'd be really proud of you." Oscar pointed to a two-story brown brick home. It had a cute front porch on the front. "That's Potter's."

The porch had a couple of bales of hay with a few pumpkins and gourds. It was done tastefully, unlike his neighbor, who had Halloween blow-ups on every inch of the yard. There were fake bats painted on all the windows and a big skull and crossbones on the front door.

"That's so funny." I laughed as I turned the car off. "Those were the houses we loved to trick or treat at, remember?"

"I do." Oscar smiled.

We got out of the car and walked along Patch's sidewalk.

Oscar knocked on the door. This had to be the hardest part for him as a sheriff.

"Sheriff. Ms. Heal." Patch opened the door. He raked his hands through his hair to try to get his bed head to calm down. He yawned, "It's pretty early for a social call."

"Patch, this isn't the kind of visit I like to make." Oscar looked around. The morning was about to break wide open and Patch's life was about to change forever.

Patch's face stilled. He looked at Oscar and then at me.

"Can we come inside?" Oscar asked.

"Sure." Patch opened the door. As we stepped across the threshold, he asked, "Is something wrong with the pumpkin patch?"

He shut the door behind us.

Oscar took his sheriff's hat off and held it under his arm.

"I'm sorry to say that we found Patty's body lying over one of your pumpkins this morning." Oscar's voice drifted off.

"I told him to stop drinking." Patch shook his head. "Do you have him in a cell so he can wear off the drunk?"

"Patch, I'm sorry, Patty is dead." Oscar made himself a little clearer.

"Dead?" Patch leaned forward and lowered his voice.

"Unfortunately, until the autopsy comes back, we won't know for sure what happened, but it looks like someone killed him." Oscar straightened his shoulders. "Without an official report, we are looking at it as a murder as it appears he was stabbed multiple times...someone used him as a pin cushion."

"Patch, a voodoo doll was found at the scene, so we think someone from the spiritual community killed him," I stepped up and ran a hand down his arm. "I'm so sorry, but we'd like to ask a few questions if we can."

"Sure." Patch shook his head as if he were trying to fix all the rattling going around inside his mind. "I'm just not sure." He looked up at me with watery eyes. "I'm not sure why anyone would kill him. Yeah, he is brash. Was brash," his voiced trailed. "Oh, God!"

Oscar grabbed Patch as his body slumped down to the floor. Oscar looked up at me.

"I'll go see if there is some coffee to put on." I didn't like seeing grown men so upset, so I excused myself to go find the kitchen and let Oscar do what he was trained to do.

I couldn't help but peek inside each door as I walked down the hallway making my way down to the large open room I could see at the end, which was probably a family room adjacent to the kitchen.

I pushed open the doors and took a quick peek inside. One of the rooms had a messed up bed, so I figured that one was Patch's. Another room was a bathroom. And the other room was a bedroom where the bed was still made and there was a suitcase on the floor.

I looked back over my shoulder and could hear Oscar consoling Patch, but didn't see them following me. I walked inside and did a quick scan of the room to see if there was anything I could find or something that would alert me to why someone would want Patty dead. Namely any of my friends.

On the table next to the bed was a half full glass of water beside a photo of younger versions of Patty and Ophelia, both wearing a uniform. I picked it up and took a closer look. They were standing in front of a building and other people with variations of the uniform were behind them, but not part of the picture. It was like someone had snapped their photo together. Both of them smiling at the camera.

I slipped the photo into my jeans pocket when I heard Oscar's voice a little closer. My intuition tugged and told me to get out of there. I hurried down the hall where I noted I had been right, the big room was a large family room with a vaulted wood-beam ceiling and the back wall was shaped in an A-frame with floor-to-ceiling windows with the perfect view of the pumpkin patch.

"Nice view." I realized it wasn't probably the right thing to say when Patch and Oscar walked in, but I had sincerely meant it.

"Yes. I picked this lot for that reason. I knew when the Order of Elders opened up the village to new businesses, that I had to be part of it. Especially in Kentucky with all the seasons. It's perfect to grow pumpkins," Patch said.

"Where is your coffee?" I asked and walked over to the kitchen.

The cabinets were grey and the countertop was concrete. His house was very masculine and fit his personality.

"In the cabinet above the coffee pot." He sloppily gestured. "Just make yourself at home."

He eased himself on one of the stools at the high top counter and Oscar sat down next to him.

"Do you have any clues who might've done this?" Patch propped his elbow up on the counter and held up his head with his hand.

"That's how I'm hoping you can help." Oscar began to ask his questions while I found all the stuff to make the pot of coffee. "Do you know anyone who might've wanted to hurt him?"

"He has a big mouth. There are plenty of times he's gotten himself into scuffles when he should've let stuff roll off his back. But you saw him with Colton." He shrugged.

"Why would he and Colton have gotten into a fight?" I asked and leaned my backside against the concrete countertop, folding my arms.

"They had gone to the wizard academy together. Didn't you go?" he asked Oscar.

"Actually, I didn't. But tell me about their time there." Oscar and I both had had no idea we were spiritualists until we were adults, so we got the fast track education. Oscar took out a pad of paper and began to jot down what Patch was saying.

"Colton's father and my father were both police officers and had gone to the academy together as young boys. They were very competitive and Colton's father got the Medal of Valor."

"What's that?" I asked.

"It's the highest medal awarded to one student in the academy. That student gets to pick whatever spiritual community they want to run. As a stab to my family and from the competition with my father, Colton's father picked our family's spiritual community in the west." Patch bit the edges of his lip. "He did it purely out of spite. He could've picked anywhere. But he didn't. He wanted to have more competition with my father. My father had to work under him as a deputy. My father had terrible working hours. Got the worst cases. It was a nightmare. But my father had to stick with it since it was our only income and he had sent Patty and me to the best boarding school."

"Is that where you met Ophelia Biblio?" I asked.

The coffee pot beeped that it was finished and I searched the other cabinet next to the coffee pot to retrieve the mugs.

He continued as I poured three cups of coffee, "Yes. It was apparent that the competition didn't just stop with my father and Mr. Lance." Patch reached for the cup as I set it down. He curled his hands around it. "Mr. Lance had heard where we were going to school and he enrolled Colton there as well."

Oscar and I sipped our coffee as the story unfolded, giving Colton a motive to kill.

"Not only did Colton win the Medal of Valor, but he also won Ophelia's heart." Patch twisted his body to look out over the pumpkin patch beyond the windows.

"You mean to tell me that Patty and Ophelia were a couple?" I asked.

"They weren't just a couple. They were engaged. Ring, dress, date and all." He turned back around. The corners of his eyes dipped along with his lips. "It was more of a family arrangement but Patty was head over heels in love with her but she wasn't in love with him. Don't get me wrong. They were good friends and had a great time, but the day Colton showed up, Patty said he could see it in her eyes that she was smitten."

"So your family lost out again to the Lances." Oscar was putting together the puzzle pieces of the past and a reason for murder.

"If you'll excuse me. I think I need to go to the bathroom. I think I'm going to be sick." Patch jumped up and headed back down the hall.

"Are you thinking what I'm thinking?" Oscar asked. I flinched at the tone of his voice.

I pushed myself off the counter and walked over to the bar where Oscar was sitting. I leaned over and whispered, "Did Patty go see Ophelia at Ever After and try to steal her back? Make her confused since she isn't married to Colton and that's why she asked Colton for some space? Colton figured out or she told him that Patty was in town and that's. . ."

"A reason for Colton to murder him," Oscar finished my sentence. His voice was absolutely devoid of any emotion and it chilled me.

Chapter Nine

The town was abuzz with the news of Patty Potter's death. Even though he wasn't a citizen, it was still hard for everyone to process that there had been a murder. Word spread fast in the small spiritual village.

"Good morning," I tried to put on a cheery face when customers walked through the door.

Since Petunia was the Village President, she got in touch with the shop owners to let them know it was business as usual and the police had everything under control. She knew as well as I did that Oscar had no idea who'd done this, but there were suspects and motives.

My thoughts swirled around to Ophelia. I couldn't imagine her killing anyone, but the creepy conversation I'd overheard her and Patty having in the woods gave her motive. If he wasn't going to leave her alone, she had motive to force him to.

"Excuse me," the customer waved her hand in front of my face.

"I'm so sorry." I blinked. "I haven't had enough coffee this morning. How can I help you?"

"My doctor said I've got a rotator cuff problem." The woman did windmills in the middle of the shop. When she turned to face the light, I noticed it was Hazel Jones.

Mr. Prince Charming ran underneath the table, the tip of his white tail stuck out from underneath the red tablecloth.

"Hazel." My face spread into a smile. "Welcome to my shop. I met you last night. June Heal."

Hazel squinted her eyes. She returned the smile. "Oh, honey. Of course, you are married to that hunky police officer of our town."

"I sure am." It was so refreshing to see new faces living in the village.

The spry old woman didn't waste any time getting down to business.

"Now, if it was a rotator cuff, I don't think I could do this." She wind-milled her arms the other way.

"May I?" I reached out to touch her arm.

She didn't hesitate. She jutted her arm out and pulled up her sleeve.

"I'm not a doctor or anything." I put my hands around her arm.

My intuition took over and a strong smell of roses curled around my nose. I moved my hands up her arm and grazed her shoulder.

"Sometimes I hate to see summer end." I gazed at her. "I have the prettiest rose garden at my home and sometimes it makes me sad to see them die in the fall."

"I have a rose garden." She squealed and rolled down her sleeve. "I work in it all day long."

"I love working in mine." I rubbed my deltoid muscle. "Sometimes I get really sore about here."

"That's where my pain is. The doctor said it's radiating from the rotator cuff and wants me to get a MRI." She shook her head. "I'd heard about your shop and decided to come see if you got any homeopathic stuff to try before I go under the knife."

"We don't want that to happen, do we." I smiled and took the bottle from her hands. "I'll be right back."

I glanced around the shop to make sure everyone was okay. I was more than happy to disappear behind my partition and concoct a potion for my customer. It was a great distraction from what had taken place a couple hours earlier. I snagged my apron off the hook next to the counter and put it on.

Mr. Prince Charming jumped up next to the cauldron and watched as I ran my hand down the ingredient shelf. The Calendula glowed, letting me know it was the perfect ingredient to add to my potion for Hazel's pulled deltoid. It was a wonderful homeopathic ingredient to help heal wounds.

I sprinkled a dash of the orange ingredient into the cauldron. The thick murky liquid rolled to a boil. The ladle stirred in a counter-clockwise circle three times before changing course to stir in a clockwise circle.

The moving liquid deep in the cauldron swirled the potion to a pink with red accretions on the bottom. It smelled of the most fragrant roses.

"Hmmm." I took a nice long whiff. It was one of the most fragrant potions I could remember. I smiled, knowing how much Hazel was going to benefit from the special potion.

This was one of the main reasons I loved being a witch. To actually be able to help people with their real problems.

The bell over the door dinged and I stuck my head out from behind the partition to see Faith making her way back to the counter, only to be stopped by Hazel.

I put a sprinkle of Bellis perennis in the cauldron for good measure. As it aids in healing cuts and wounds it would give Hazel a boost to her immune system, not that she needed it.

The baby blue bottle from the shelf glowed. The pink butterfly on the bottle lit up and sparkled, letting me know it was the perfect bottle for Hazel's potion.

Gingerly, I picked it up off the shelf and smiled. I remembered the day the bottle appeared and I had wondered who the special bottle was meant for.

My eyes slid down the shelf, taking in all the bottles that had appeared in my life. Some days there were more bottles appearing than I had space for, but if they showed up, then I knew they were for me to use on someone special.

When I made a special potion for someone, the bottle that was intended for that potion and that person aligned and would glow so I knew it was meant to be.

I uncorked the top and let it dangle from the brown cord attached to the neck of the bottle and held the bottle over top of the cauldron, allowing the potion to magically transfer from the cauldron to the bottle.

I quickly grabbed the spray bottle that held the cauldron cleaner and spritzed the inside so it would be ready for the next time I needed it.

"I see that you two have met." I walked around the counter where Faith and Hazel were still chatting.

"Yes, we were just getting acquainted." Faith looked at me. "Did you know that Hazel lives in the new development?"

"I did. We met last night." I held the pretty butterfly bottle to her. "She's got a rotator cuff issue and her doctor said she might need surgery, but we are going to try rubbing this on morning and night. All over your shoulder, down your arm and under your armpit."

Hazel repeated the direction.

"Don't worry." I stuck my hand in the front pocket of my apron and pulled out a card with instructions that just so happened to appear as I need them. I loved how that happened. "Here are the directions in case you forget."

"Can I take your photo for the art gallery?" Faith asked.

Hazel proudly held the bottle up to her face and smiled real big for the camera as Faith clicked away.

"Now, you two need to come by and see my rose garden. I'll make up a pitcher of tea." Hazel paid me for the potion. "Stop by anytime. No need to call!"

Faith and I waved Hazel goodbye.

"I'm so glad you are here." I glanced around the shop to make sure no customers needed me. I motioned for Faith to follow me behind the counter. "I heard your report in the paper about Patty."

Since Petunia had notified everyone, I knew everyone knew and it could be discussed outside of Oscar's pending investigation.

"It's terrible," she said. "But he was a little nasty. He threatened me to stop taking pictures."

"Really?" I asked as if I hadn't already known. "Why?"

"Didn't you hear him at the fight between him and Colton?" She shook her head. "He was so mad."

"Oh that's what you meant when he threatened you?" I asked again to make sure.

"Yeah. I guess he didn't want anyone to see him fighting. But I'm sick over Colton." She shook her head.

"What do you mean?" I asked.

"You can't tell me that Oscar doesn't think Colton is who killed Patty." She drew back and held the camera snug to her chest.

"I don't know. You know Oscar." I pish-poshed her thinking. "He doesn't tell me anything that goes on outside of the office."

"You'd better get going." Faith tapped the watch on her wrist. "You are going to be late for your own smudging."

I looked up at the clock on the wall and noticed it was already time for the council meeting.

"I figured I'd watch the shop so you didn't have to close." She walked around me and put the camera down on the counter.

"You are right." I was thankful for Faith being there to help out. She was a great part-time employee. I untied the apron and hung it up. "Do you really think Colton killed him?"

"Absolutely." Her quick-to-judge answer rang deep in my soul. "What?"

I didn't have a very good poker face.

"I don't know." I grabbed my smudging materials from underneath the counter and stuck them in my bag. "Patty and Colton had words, but I just don't see Colton as the killer."

Though I had the information about Patty and Colton's history, my intuition told me there was more to the story. By no means was it telling me that Colton didn't do it, but it also wasn't jabbing me to say he did.

"From what I heard," Faith leaned in. "Ophelia was leaving Colton for Patty."

"Who did you hear that from?" I was curious as to where the gossip mill had started.

"You tell me." Faith shrugged and began to straighten the bottles on the display table in front of the counter. "I heard you were with her last night."

"Gerald?" My brows lifted. He was the only person who saw us last night.

"Gerald?" Faith *tsked*. "He'd be the last person to gossip."

"Then who?" I asked.

"Patty Porter." Her eyes darkened.

"June," the voice called from the door of the shop. It was Chandra Shango from the shop next door, A Cleansing Spirit Spa. "Do you want to go together?"

A cool morning breeze shuffled a few leaves across the floor. Mr. Prince Charming scurried across the room and batted at them as if he were playing a game.

She referred to the council meeting. We usually left our shops the same time and walked up the hill together.

"You talked to Patty last night after he got into a fight with Colton?" I asked.

Faith nodded her head.

"Well?" Chandra stuck her hands on her hips, hiking up the side of her cloak.

"I'll be back." I held my finger up in the air. "And I want to hear everything he had to say."

"I've got you covered." Faith walked over to another table and straightened more of the displays.

There was a purple mist that hung over the mountainous background. The sun was trying to burst through to give a little warmth to the crisp fall day.

"I think I need to hire someone." Chandra made simple conversation. "I've been so busy and having these meetings in the middle of the day makes me close down and I simply can't afford to have that reputation with the new citizens."

Reputation? Her word struck a chord with my intuition.

"Chandra." I kissed her on the cheek on our way up the hill to The Gathering Rock. "You are a genius!"

Colton and Ophelia might be the obvious suspects, but that was too obvious for me. I couldn't forget the fight I had heard between the brothers and Oscar didn't seem to take that into consideration. He assumed it was just a tiff between brothers. But a tiff didn't involve words *over my dead body* as Patch had promised.

I was definitely going to stop by and see Patch again. This time alone and try to figure out what exactly their brotherly love consisted of.

"Good afternoon." I smiled at the village council members that included Petunia, Gerald, and Izzy, while Chandra joined them.

They stood at the front of The Gathering Rock. I placed my smudging items next to the rock and got them set up so when all the members of our spiritual community showed up, we were ready to go. I was on a mission to get back to the shop and see exactly what Faith had to say and then make another trip over to the new development.

"June, may I speak with you for a moment?" KJ appeared next to me. He stood in his traditional headdress and loin cloth clothing I was used to seeing him in. He tilted his head to the side and slowly walked into the wooded area next to The Gathering Rock space.

The ceremony wasn't ready to begin and there were spiritualists still climbing the hill, so I walked over to him.

He pulled a smudge stick from underneath his loin cloth and jerked a feather from his headdress.

"The time has passed." He held them out for me to take. "The connection between the people and our plants are lost. There is discord within our spiritual community. We are losing our spiritual connection to Turtle Island."

I knew from the past, he was referring to America but calling it Turtle Island because it was his native tongue.

"The importance of what you and I do with our herbs and homeopathic cures can help bring peace and harmony while we are going through the change of growth. Please consider doing a smudging for every person at the meeting." His voice was disciplined and maintained complete control though my insides were a jittery mess.

I sucked in a deep breath as I reached out to take his smudge stick and feather. I glanced over his shoulder and noticed there were a lot of spiritualists gathered in the space.

"This is going to take a while." I wasn't sure how much time we were going to need, but I did know that if I had to smudge every single person, it would go well into the afternoon.

"I think a little more time to save our culture and world is worth it. Don't you?" he asked, but didn't wait for my answer. He simply turned and walked back to the meeting space leaving me as his words hung in the air in front of me.

When I first started to do the smudging ceremony, I wasn't really sure how to do it. I was told that I needed to rely on my intuition to guide me. I did that and it didn't let me down. It never has and I knew more than ever that I was going to have to rely on that gift now.

I dragged the smudge stick under my nose and let the smells pass through my nose and down into my soul. I closed my eyes and held my breath as the scent seeped deep into my soul and my being.

My intuition took over and I knew exactly what I needed to do.

"Good afternoon." I held the smudge stick up in the air letting everyone know that I was about to start the sacred ceremony. "Please gather in a circle."

I walked into the middle.

"This is a cedar smudge ceremony." I referred to the bundle KJ had given me. My intuition told me it was cedar. "Cedar is a medicine of protection. Cedar trees are very old, wise and powerful spirits. Since we have new citizens joining our spiritual community, I'd like to use this ceremony to help with moving in, inviting unwanted spirits to leave and protecting each one of us and our places or objects from unwanted influences."

I lit the bundle setting it on fire and let the flame grow taller and taller as the black smoke started to curl in the sky. With a few swipes of the feather in the smoke, I twirled, fanning the protection to the north, south, east and west before brushing a few strokes to Mother Earth, the ground.

With the bundle and feather, I walked over to Petunia who was the Village President and first in the circle.

"Place your hand over your heart." I instructed her.

"June, are you doing everyone?" she asked in a whisper.

"Place your hand over your heart." It was as if her words didn't register as my intuition took over and the words fell from my lips.

I looked into Petunia's eyes for a moment to "greet" her and let her know I came in peace. I fanned the smoke at her heart and then up to the right side of her head. I took a step back as a bird flew from Petunia's messy up-do before I walked around her, clockwise, gently washing her body in the smoke of the cedar.

I continued to brush the smoke down over her left shoulder and the length of her arm and back up again to her shoulder before I moved to the left side of her torso.

Using the feather I dragged the smoke up her left leg and foot, smoothly dragging it over to her right foot, up the right leg, torso and down the length of the right arm and back up to her shoulder.

I turned Petunia around to her right and repeated these movements as I smudged the back of her all while I chanted, "I welcome the energy of within, the principle of being connected, the energy and spirit of within. I welcome the gifts of balance, oneness, and the connection with all things, for all things are one and all things are related."

The smoke billowed around her and circled her like a tornado. It darted straight up into the sky in a fluid motion.

"Ho!" I flung the feather at her face as the last bit of smoke dissipated.

Chapter Ten

No matter how fast I went, it seemed like it took forever to smudge each person at the meeting. It was great to see all the new members of our spiritual community, including Violet and Gene, the mother and son duo Oscar and I had met on our honeymoon.

"Order!" Petunia banged the gavel on the table that was placed in front of The Gathering Rock.

There were folding chairs set up in front of them for all of us to sit. Everyone hurried to find a seat as Petunia began to read off the docket.

"First I would like to welcome all the new shop owners." She pushed a falling stick from her hair back into it, sending a few dried leaves out the other side. "Hidden Treasures is owned by Violet Draper. Violet's son Gene is also a new member of our community. Gene will be attending Hidden Halls in a couple of weeks. Violet is a Cyclomancy spiritualist."

I looked over with a smile on my heart. Violet was a wonderful mother, but I knew Gene was going to love Hidden Halls and I couldn't wait to talk to him about it. Plus, it was exciting to have a Cyclomancer among us. Hidden Treasures, her consignment and clothing shop, was a perfect cover for her gift.

"Scented Swan Candles is owned by Chandler Swan." When Petunia called his name, Chandler stood up and waved to the group. "Chandler's spiritual gift is Ceromancy."

Another exciting gift I thought as the excitement bubbled up inside me. It was going to be great having these new merchants and new friends. Chandler was able to melt wax or simply gaze into a flame of a burning candle to interpret what he saw into prophecy. Fascinating.

"Cherry Merry owns Blue Moon Gallery along with her brother Perry. Our very own Faith Mortimer will have her first photography viewing over the All Hallows' Eve week. Be sure to stop by." Petunia leaned over as Gerald whispered something. "Oh, Cherry and Perry are both Psychometry spiritualists."

This caught my attention. This means that she can form impressions that may come in the form of emotions, sounds, scents, tastes or images. A gallery was a pretty cool shop and a perfect way to cover up her gift.

"Please welcome Leah LeRoy." Petunia must really like her because she gave her a clap. "I personally am excited because Leah owns Crazy Crafty Chick and has invited all of us to ceramic night tomorrow night. I'm going to be making a cute cat with a witch's hat for Halloween. So please join us in front of the shop tomorrow night at ten pm."

"Yes, please come." Leah greeted everyone and smiled. "I'm a Clairsentience and thrilled to be part of the village."

A Clairsentience was able to pick up on sensations and art was a wonderful way to do that.

"And we are thrilled to welcome a longtime friend to our village, KJ." All the council smiled as everyone looked over at him. "He's just like family around here and he owns Happy Herb. He is a Native American Spiritualist that has exactly what you need for any potions, spells, scents," Petunia shrugged, "anything."

KJ waved and smiled. It was such a joy to have him here.

"Unfortunately, our last shop owner isn't able to attend." Petunia stood up. Everyone's eyes were on her.

"Patch Potter owns Potter's Pumpkin Patch. Even though the pumpkin patch is really only open to the public during peak autumn hours, he is also the head farmer of the new agri-hood. I'm sorry to remind you that Patch's twin brother Patty was found deceased in the pumpkin patch early this morning. I'm expecting the Karima sisters to be here any minute to give us a preliminary report on the autopsy along with Sheriff Oscar Park."

"We are here." Oscar appeared with the Karima sisters next to him. "We are currently going to investigate Patty Potter's death as a homicide. I currently have Sheriff Colton Lance at the station for questioning and we are asking any of you to come forward if you have seen or heard anything that might help in bringing the killer to justice."

An audible gasp waved across the community members. A few of them leaned into their neighbor and whispered.

"Is it true a wand was stuck in his side?" Chandler seemed a bit too interested in the gory details.

"There was." Constance Karima waddled up in front of Oscar.

"There was." Patience joined her. She pushed her glasses up on the bridge of her nose and looked at her sister.

"The wand was just a cover as it didn't puncture any vital organs to cause death." Constance looked at Patience. Patience smiled at her sister.

"No vital organs." Patience nodded.

"We found traces of boric acid in his system. Of course this is just a preliminary test." Constance was interrupted by her sister.

"Mmmhmmm, preliminary." Patience giggled.

Constance gave her the stink eye before she turned back to the crowd.

"This means that somehow he ingested it and they tried to cover it up with the wands," she finished.

"If that's the case, why is Colton in custody if the wand didn't kill him?" Gene chirped from his seat in the front. "I mean, my mom took me to the pumpkin patch and I saw that murdered man yell at the woman with the camera too."

"You are going to make a fine wizard." Oscar discounted him which made me pause. Gene had a good point.

"This is an ongoing investigation. I'm just holding Sheriff Lance for questioning. Again, I'm asking any of you to come forward with any information you might have even if you don't think it will help with the investigation." Oscar looked over at Izzy.

"Thank you Sheriff Park for the update." Izzy planted her hands on the table in front of her. "I'd like to talk to you about the new agri-hood and the findings of the Order of Elders." Izzy Solstice stood up. She pushed back her long blond wavy hair before she rubbed her hands down her black a-frame skirt with small pumpkins dotted all over it. "As many of you know, Locust Grove owns all the land around us and had development plans for the new neighborhood. There has been a lot of interest in our land bringing much, too much, attention to our way of living. The Order of Elders felt it was important to get the heat off of us, so we might as well join them. I know we can keep our world a secret from them and our lives separate. Our meetings will have to be late at night, but most of us work well at night. A witch hunt is the last thing we need."

Witch hunt? I gulped. Ophelia's words *we are becoming a dying breed* stabbed at my intuition. I reached into my bag and dug down deep to grab my June's Gem as incomplete thoughts swirled around my head.

Chapter Eleven

The council passed Faith's proposal for a physical paper version of the *Whispering Falls Gazette* for the mortals while she would still deliver the paper to the spiritualists through the air. I tried to follow along but my mind was wrapped around other things. Like the dying breed statement.

What exactly did that mean? Did Patty know something that we didn't and that's why he was killed? Did Ophelia know something?

"That was a long meeting." Oscar walked up next to me as Violet and Gene joined us.

"Hi, buddy." Oscar raked his hand across Gene's head and mussed up his hair. "This is for you." Oscar pulled out a sheriff's badge paper sticker that he gave out to all the kids in Locust Grove.

Gene tugged on Oscar's sleeve.

"You said to report anything big or small." Gene's small voice was quickly silenced by Violet.

"Gene, you have taken up enough of Oscar and June's time back on Tulip Island." She laughed. "He wants to be an officer, if you haven't already noticed."

"You'll make a fine officer." Oscar winked. "I hear you are going to school at Hidden Halls."

Gene nodded with his lips tucked together.

"June and I went there and you are going to love it." Oscar continued to talk as I bent down to get my smudge items together.

"*Psst.*" The sputter of lips got my attention. "*Psst.*"

I looked around The Gathering Rock as I collected the smudging pack and noticed a flutter of leaves swirling in the woods. I sucked in a deep breath and glanced around me. Oscar and Violet were engrossed with talking to Gene so they wouldn't notice if I walked into the woods.

"June," Ophelia's eyes were bright. She looked scared. "I'm going to take you up on your offer to stay in your home in Locust Grove."

"Okay." My brows furrowed. There was a numbness to her as if her feelings were paralyzed.

"Like now?" she asked. Mr. Prince Charming appeared from behind her. "He's been keeping me company." She shrugged, a weak smile curled on the edges of her lips.

I looked down at my fairy-god cat. He was doing figure eights around Ophelia's ankles, letting me know it was a good idea to take her.

"Come on." I flung my bag across my torso and headed through the wooded area to the west so we'd be covered by the trees, dense as they were this time of the year.

The wooded area ran along the back of my cottage and I knew we could get there without being seen, but my El Camino would be seen leaving my house.

The snap of a branch cracked in the distance. Ophelia and I stopped, looking at each other with wide open eyes.

"Please," she begged in a whisper. There was a scared plea in her tone. "I'm begging you to get me out of here."

I grabbed her hand and we took off toward the house. Mr. Prince Charming darted ahead of us giving us the easiest and fastest trail. We stopped once we made it to the back of the cottage. I dug down into my bag and grabbed my keys. Without a word I held them up and gave her the nod once Mr. Prince Charming darted to the Green Machine.

After we got into the car, I started it. Mr. Prince Charming jumped up on the dash and took his usual spot. Once we were settled I put the shift in drive and headed down the hill and out of town without looking in the rear view mirror.

If Oscar saw me and I saw him, my guilt would want me to stop and let him know what I was doing, especially since he did lead me to believe he wanted to talk to Ophelia. According to the by-laws, any spiritualist who was a suspect in a crime was not allowed to leave Whispering Falls until the crime was solved.

"Thank you." Ophelia spoke as the wooden sign on the side of the road that posted we were leaving Whispering Falls darted past us. "I know that you probably just went against Oscar's wishes."

"I didn't." I dragged my bag into my lap and dug my hand down into it and grabbed two June's Gems, handing her one. If I ever needed a stress relief, it was now. "He never once named you a suspect, though I do believe that he wanted to. In fact, my intuition tells me that Colton might've swayed Oscar from bringing you in."

"I'm telling you right now that Colton didn't kill Patty." Her words were bitter and sharp. She took a bite of her June's Gem.

"Did you?" Yep, I went there.

"No!" she yelled through a mouthful of chocolate. "I'd never kill Patty even though I wanted to years ago."

"Can you tell me what happened between the three of you when you were in boarding school?" I asked and headed straight out of town.

Mr. Prince Charming remained sitting and staring out the windshield. His body moved with the curves of the old country road between Whispering Falls and Locust Grove.

"I really want to tell you, but I can't." She lowered her head. Her fingers fiddled with the half-eaten Gem.

"I can't help Colton or you for that matter if you can't come clean with me," I pointed out and gripped the wheel with both hands after I stuck the rest of the Gem in my mouth, hoping to get a stress relief.

"I'm sworn." Her words disappeared into the air. "Just trust me when I tell you that Colton didn't do it. And I don't want to leave him. But I have to."

"Okay." I held tighter to the wheel so as not to lose my cool. "You said something that really struck a chord with me last night."

"What?" she asked, looking over at me.

"You said that we were a dying breed." I glanced over at her. On the curve, the moon penetrated the windshield and cast a shadow down her face. "Oh my God." I gasped. "Are you a Dark-Sider?"

Ophelia said nothing and the silence hung between us as I thought about the implications. There was nothing worse than the betrayal of a best friend. The day Ophelia Biblio moved to Whispering Falls, she portrayed herself as something she obviously wasn't. I'm not saying a Dark-Sider was a bad spiritualist. Even though according to the past, they weren't the easiest going. But Raven Mortimer and Eloise are Dark-Siders and they are amazing.

"June, you haven't said a word the entire twenty-minute drive." Ophelia broke the silence once we pulled up to my family home on the outskirts of Locust Grove.

"I'm hurt." I slammed the gear into park and adjusted myself in the seat to face her. "When you and Colton came to Whispering Falls with Alise." I'd totally forgotten about Colton's mom being with them. "You knew I was Village President at the time and I had just transitioned the community of Whispering Falls from a Good-Sider community only to a more diverse village, accepting Dark-Siders."

After I'd met the Mortimer sisters, I knew that Whispering Falls was missing out on some good residents, so the first thing I did as president was to amend the law to incorporate everyone in the spiritual community.

"You knew that, so I'm not sure why you have kept your heritage a secret. Especially with me." The hurt run deep to my toes.

Many times I'd confided in Ophelia and many times had Oscar confided in Colton.

"I'm not saying I'm not going to tell you everything," her voice cracked. "I just need time to think about it. And you allowing me to stay here will help me do that."

"Does your secret with Patty have anything to do with you being a Dark-Sider?" My gut told me I was on the right track.

She nodded.

"Please let me tell you on my own time." Her eyes dragged up to mine. "Please promise me you will do everything in your power to figure out who killed Patty and get Colton off the hook."

I stared at her.

"Promise me," she begged.

"I promise." I wasn't sure if I'd just made a deal with my new enemy or my old best friend.

Chapter Twelve

The smell of freshly brewed coffee wafted through the house, tickling my nose. Or at least I thought it was tickling my nose.

When I opened my eyes, Mr. Prince Charming was standing on top of me, dragging his tail under my nose. Oscar was sitting on the edge of my side of the bed with a cup of steaming coffee waiting for me in his hand.

"I wanted to make sure I saw you before I went to work today." He handed me the cup of joe as I pushed myself up to sitting.

"Thank you." I accepted the warming kiss on the lips right after Mr. Prince Charming jumped off of me.

"I'm not going to ask you where you took Ophelia last night because I have a pretty good idea." He was on to me. "But I am going to ask you to tell me anything pertinent to the case if it involves her."

"I can't tell you much because *she* didn't tell *me* much, but I can tell you that she claims neither she nor Colton killed Patty." I knew it wasn't much to give him, it wasn't much for me to go on either, but it was what I knew.

I did leave out the Dark-Sider part because I wanted to get in touch with Alise and she see if she knew something. I had her name and address since she was a client of A Charming Cure. She had me ship items to her regularly.

"Colton swears up and down he didn't do it and in the light of the boric acid discovery, I had a better idea of what to look for, but didn't find any evidence of it in Ever After Books." Oscar had obviously gone through the bookstore with a fine-tooth comb since Colton and Ophelia did live there.

"If what she says is true and they had nothing to do with it, then someone certainly is trying to make me believe they did." He pulled out his phone from his pocket. It was a note from the note section of his phone. "I have a sworn witness statement that says they saw Patty and Ophelia walk off together the night he died. They walked into the woods."

I read what was on his phone.

"Who was the witness?" I asked.

"I can't tell you that. It's part of the open investigation." He wasn't budging.

"Not even for a kiss?" I asked.

"Not even for a kiss." He grinned. "But I do have a little time before I have to go into work."

He drew me in his arms.

An hour later, I was off and running down the hill to the shop, where I was going to be late opening up for the day. I had really wanted to stop by Wicked Good and put a bug in Raven's ear about the argument Faith had had with Patty, but it would have to wait.

Or not.

As soon as I opened the door to A Charming Cure, Faith was inside working on the display tables.

"Hi." Her chipper voice rang out in the empty shop. "I wasn't sure if you needed me this morning or not."

"I'm a little surprised to see you." I walked over to the counter and hung my cloak up on the hook and set my bag on the counter.

"You are?" Faith's big blue eyes stared back at me. "Why?"

I walked back to the front door of the shop and flipped the sign to open. I noticed the table of goodies and treats Faith had set up next to the door.

"I'm sorry." I shook my head and looked at the cauldron-shaped crock-pot she'd put apple cider in to simmer and the cute pumpkin mugs for the customers to use. There were a plate of June's Gems that were in the shape of pumpkins and a couple of apple tarts along with brochures on the All Hallows' Eve festivities for the customers to take. My guilt set in because I knew in my heart Faith could never hurt a soul. "I'm having a hard time coming up with who would want Patty dead."

"Well it wasn't me if that what's going on inside of that head of yours." Faith walked through the store and tugged on the edges of the display tablecloths so they were straight and wrinkle free. "Just because he got angry at me for taking his picture gives me no reason to kill him."

"You're right." I bit the edges of my lips.

"Now Colton, he's a different story." She ran her fingers down the wall display and turned all the potion bottles around so the labels were facing out. "I don't know why, but he was going to beat Patty to death. Didn't you see his eyes?" There was a chill in her voice.

"I didn't. It all happened so fast." I sucked in a deep breath.

"I can't wait to see my photos displayed at Blue Moon Gallery because not only did I probably get a good one of the fight," she paused and smiled, "I caught a spiritual love connection later after the fight."

"What?" I wrinkled my nose. "Who?" I asked and walked over to help her finish tidying up the shop because I saw a couple customers walking up the shop steps.

The bell rang their arrival.

"Good morning," I greeted the two women. "Please help yourself to some hot cider and a pastry this fall morning."

The women scurried over to the goodie table which gave me time to pump Faith for some much needed gossip to get my mind away from the murder.

"Patch Potter and Violet Draper." Faith made kissy noises.

"Oh," I shoo'ed her. "That can't be." I shook my head.

Faith nodded. "I'm telling you, it is brewing." She tapped her ears, which probably meant she heard it in a breeze.

"He's not her type. Trust me. When Oscar and I were on our honeymoon, I saw and met Gene's dad. A mortal hunk." I leaned in to whisper so the customers wouldn't hear me, "I'm mean hot hunk, not Patch Potter cute."

"Maybe she's changing her taste in men. But I'm telling you, there could be another wedding on the horizon." She grinned and excused herself to help one of the customers.

It wasn't the gossip about the possible romance between Patch and Violet that sat on my mind all day long, it was the fact that Faith said she had taken pictures the night Patty was killed after the fight. The activity in the shop had been nonstop with customers and I'd made my fair share of extra potions as Faith continued to help customers with everyday homeopathic products like lotions, bath salts, antacids, and other home remedies.

Before I knew it, it was lunchtime and I'd yet to have breakfast. I did count coffee as its own food group, but it wasn't enough to sustain me all day.

"I'll go grab us lunch from The Gathering Grove." I glanced around the shop and noticed it was a perfect time to leave, grab lunch and check in with Cherry Merry to see if they'd started to put up Faith's gallery.

"Perfect. I'll take a BLT on rye with a cup of his chili." There was a distinct pleasure on Faith's face. She was right. Gerald did make good chili.

I grabbed my bag and strapped it across my body before retrieving my cloak off the hook and throwing it around me. Every time someone opened the shop door, the cool breeze drifted in even though the sun was shining.

Mr. Prince Charming and I ran across the street, darting in and out of traffic to get to The Gathering Grove. One thing was for sure. Since we opened up the village to mortal living, traffic had increased as well as business.

All of the café tables along the front of the tea shop were filled with smiling customers and steaming bowls of soups and warm drinks. In the middle of the tables, Gerald had put an All Hallows' Eve flyer in a plastic photo frame along with a stack for customers to take one.

Everything would be perfect if it weren't for the pall of the murder investigation of Patty Potter. All the shops were excited. The pumpkin patch was an added bonus and the shop windows were all decorated. I loved the large coffee cup surrounded by leaves that Gerald had painted on his windows. He didn't have the extra space in the shop to build a big display like A Charming Cure. He had to use that space for more customer tables, so he was very inventive with this window paintings.

"June!" Gerald waved from one of the tables as he cleared the dishes.

"Hi." I waved back and we moseyed on over to him. "You are busy."

"Crazy." He muffled under his mustache. He dropped the rag on the table and gestured for me to sit down as he took a seat. He curled the edge of his mustache with his finger. "Does Oscar have any leads on who murdered Patty Potter?"

Mr. Prince Charming jumped up on the table and Gerald snarled. I ignored him.

"I don't think so. Or at least I haven't heard." I let out a deep sigh. "Obviously Colton Lance is the main suspect and Oscar has him down at the station doing filing and odd jobs, but outside of that." I shook my head.

"I didn't want to say anything because I didn't see it, but when you were away on your honeymoon, Petunia had several meetings with people from Locust Grove about how they were going to tie in the police department with the new development since it was both in their city and our village." He waved and cleared his throat, "But that's not what I was going to say. Petunia said something about the pumpkin patch and the land developer having words about his house."

"What about his house?" I asked.

"She said that the developer wanted Patch to be closer to the farm land since he was the main farmer, but he insisted his house lot be next to the pumpkin patch." Gerald put his hand out to stop one of his waitresses and asked her to bring us over some afternoon tea. "That almost caused the deal to go under."

"How so?" I smiled up at the waitress and thanked her when she set the tea cup down and poured me some tea from the teapot. She set a bowl of creamer on the table in front of Mr. Prince Charming and he purred with delight as he lapped it up.

After she poured Gerald some tea, he continued while she walked away, "The developer is the one who came up with the idea of the agri-hood because he believes our village is an earthy type, Mother-Nature-loving town, if you know what I mean." His brows lifted and he took a sip of the tea.

"He's right." I shrugged. If anyone who wasn't a spiritualist came to visit Whispering Falls, they'd only find a nice, loving community of shop owners who care about the world.

"Indeed." Gerald agreed. "Obviously Patch was the best applicant for the farmer job and the development company felt that if he weren't near the farm that he'd let it go by the wayside and only tend to the pumpkin patch."

I sat back in the chair with my tea cup in my fingers taking sips as Gerald continued on.

"Petunia said they had awful words and Patch didn't like the fact that the developer accused him of not taking his job seriously, because you and I both know that we take our gifts very seriously and Patch Potter is no different." Gerald stared at me across the table.

I sat up and set my cup back on the saucer. I folded my hands and put them on the table.

"You and I both know that Patch can do both jobs with no problem too." I wiggled my brows knowing with a little help of magic anything was possible.

"The developer did everything he could to fire Patch before he even started, but the contract, with a little help of Petunia's sleight of hand, was iron-clad." His eyes narrowed. "That means they can't fire Patch unless. . ." He slid his thick pointer finger across his throat.

"But I'm not sure what this has to do with Patty," I said.

Gerald smacked his top hat with his fingers.

"June," he gasped. "Could you tell the two of them apart? I know I couldn't."

"So you are thinking that the developer killed Patty but meant to kill Patch?" I never thought of it, but I guess it could be a case of mistaken identity.

"And boric acid is used in gardens to get rid of pesky critters." He put his forearms on the table and leaned in. "Don't tell Petunia I said that or she'll be over at that farm adding critters and taking away the pesticides."

I sat back in the chair and chewed on what Gerald had said. If what he said was true and all of this happened while Oscar and I were gone, Petunia was probably so busy, it's likely she didn't remember the fight at the meeting, but Gerald did.

"From what I'm hearing from Patience Karima, whoever used him as a pin cushion was an amateur. Not a spiritualist. They wanted it to look like they knew what they were doing."

"Thanks, Gerald." I stood up. All the information fell from my brains and soaked into my body. "You might be on to something."

That something poked my intuition. It didn't make alarms go off as if it was the right track, but it definitely lit something up inside of me.

The knock at the café window made us look over. Oscar was waving and smiling.

"I'll be sure to tell Oscar." I stood up. "Can you fix me two BLT's and two bowls of your chili? I have to run up to Blue Moon so I'll be right back to get it."

"Sure thing." Gerald tipped his top hat and dragged my tea cup across the table. He looked down into it. "Who's the new romance?" he called after he read my tea leaves and Mr. Prince Charming and I headed out the door.

Chapter Thirteen

Oscar walked us down the street toward Blue Moon Gallery and Two Sisters and a Funeral. He was going to visit the Karima sisters to follow up on Patty's autopsy and I was going to make a quick stop in to see Cherry Merry.

"Gerald said all this happened during the meeting?" Oscar made notes as I told him everything Gerald had told me that Petunia had told him.

"He did. And he does have a point. Could you tell the Potter twins apart?" I asked. Mr. Prince Charming found a pile of dried leaves and plopped down, rolling all over before he found a good spot to lay.

"No." Oscar's face was blank. "Did Ophelia give you any clues to why Colton would have reason to kill Patty? Like he abused her when they knew each other? Maybe Colton was defending her honor after all these years?"

I shook my head.

"I made a promise that I'd let her get her head on straight." We climbed the hill and stopped between Two Sisters and Blue Moon. "But I can stop by the house and ask her."

"I'm going to run into Locust Grove and talk to Skip Broussert at the development company. The agri-hood was built by Broussert Developers and I know him from some police surveillance the department had done when his homes in a subdivision in Locust Grove were getting vandalized. He might be able to tell me more about that argument between him and Patch." He dragged me into a hug and kissed the top of my head. "I really want you to be careful."

"I am careful. I'm just asking questions and when I find something out I'll tell you. Just like I did with what

Gerald said." I smiled and was happy to receive a smile in return.

"Do you think if I stop by the house, Ophelia would talk to me?" he asked.

"I don't know. I told her I'd keep her whereabouts a secret and if she's not in Whispering Falls and you do name her as a suspect, she's breaking the by-laws." I chewed on my idea about contacting Alise, knowing Oscar wouldn't be happy if I left Whispering Falls without him or some backup. "I do have an idea that you probably aren't going to be to overjoyed about."

"What?" There was a little bit of curiosity in his voice tied in with apprehension.

"When Colton and Ophelia moved here, his mom was with them. I can't help but think that something in their past is keeping her and Colton apart, but I'm not sure what. I'm not even sure if Ophelia breaking up with Colton had anything to do with Patty's death, but I do know there is something there." I continued to talk as Oscar took a step back as if he was creating distance because he was about to shoot down my idea. "Hear me out before you say no."

He crossed his arms across his chest. "Go on."

"Alise is a big customer of mine and I have her address. If I take the express train to their village, I can ask her a few questions and bring up Patty. See what she says." I put my hands together and begged, "Please? What do we have to lose? I will take someone besides Mr. Prince Charming with me."

Rowl, Mr. Prince Charming didn't like that idea.

"You can go, but I'd take someone else, like. . ." I tried to think of someone on the spot that wouldn't mind going before Oscar suggested someone I'd rather not take.

"Aunt Eloise?" Oscar asked.

"Yes." I clapped my hands knowing if she would go, he'd be all over agreeing with me. Though I knew I didn't need his approval, it was nice to have.

"If she will go with you, then I have no issues. In the meantime, I'm going to check on Patty's autopsy and head on out to Broussert's office." He nodded.

"I'm going to go see if any of Faith's photos show Patty talking to anyone that might be another suspect." I tapped my stomach. "I just have a feeling we know who the killer is, but we just haven't gotten the puzzle pieces to fit."

I turned around and looked over the shops on Main Street. A dark cloud coming from the east blanketed the autumn day.

I was close. I could feel it.

"Me too." Oscar gave me one last kiss before we parted ways.

Mr. Prince Charming got up from his bed of leaves and trotted up to Blue Moon Gallery.

"Oscar!" I yelled over to Two Sisters just as he disappeared into the funeral home.

Mewl, Mr. Prince Charming purred and looked up at me.

"I wanted to tell him about what Patience had said to Gerald about the voodoo thing, but I'm sure she'll tell him while he's there." I put that in the back of my head and walked into the gallery.

Cherry Merry and Perry were both with customers so Mr. Prince Charming and I took advantage of the time and looked around. Unlike yesterday, there were big photos and painted canvases hanging from the ceiling at all different angles and lengths. There was only one that was taken at the pumpkin patch that'd been hung so far with photo credit going to Faith Mortimer. It was a perfect balance of light and color as Faith had zoomed in on a bright orange pumpkin.

There was a stack of framed photos up against the gallery wall that looked like they were next to be hung.

"Hi, June." Perry walked over. "It's fantastic. Faith has an eye for the bright and bold."

"It is lovely." I looked at Perry. "I'm here to see if there are any more she took from that night."

"Plenty. So many that Cherry was having a hard time deciding what to put on the sales floor." His eyes lit up. "We are going to make Faith our spotlight artist which means she'll have her own showing with all her photos available."

"That's wonderful." I was so happy for Faith. She'd come a long way from our days at Hidden Halls. Which reminded me to get in touch with Aunt Helena about Gene, which tickled my brain about Violet and a possible relationship with Patch.

"Excuse me." Perry exited right when I was about to ask him if I could see some more of Faith's photos. There were a ton of customers coming in and looking around.

As Mr. Prince Charming and I were about to walk out the door, Cherry called after me.

"I'm sorry we are so busy." She greeted me by kissing each side of my face, which was strange to me, but I followed suit. "Will you be at the pottery class tonight?"

"I am." I was actually looking forward to it.

"Great. We will catch up there." She smiled before she returned to her waiting customer.

I grabbed the edges of my cloak and tightened them around my neck before we darted back down the hill toward the shops.

"Well, we didn't get much out of that but at least I will be able to talk to her tonight," I said to my fairy-god cat.

Meow, he darted ahead of me and disappeared into The Gathering Grove, reminding me that I had to pick up my food.

Chapter Fourteen

After Faith and I ate our lunch, she left to go get some shots and articles together for the mortal paper version of the *Whispering Falls Gazette*. It lifted her spirits and gave her a passion I'd not seen in her for a long time and it warmed my heart.

The rest of my afternoon was spent restocking the shelves and helping out the customers. Mr. Prince Charming laid on the stool behind the counter and snoozed all afternoon.

Oscar had called and said that the autopsy was finished and the official cause of death was ingestion of boric acid. Ingestion. That made me want to throw my lunch up. I just couldn't imagine a more painful death. From what I understood, boric acid affected your nerves and that was a painful death. No matter how mean Patty was, no one deserved to die or experience a death such as that.

We made plans to meet up after the pottery class at home. He promised a fire and a glass of wine so we could wind down from our crazy day.

Though I didn't feel like I was any closer to helping him solve the murder, I was happy to get away for a few hours with my friends.

"Hi-do, June Heal." Leah's accent was so southern it nearly knocked me over. "You get on in here." She bent down and patted Mr. Prince Charming on his head. "I bet I can guess exactly what it is you are gonna make. A Halloween cat."

"We will see." I smiled and walked up on the front porch of Crazy Crafty Chick.

"You go on in and take a gander at what we are going to paint and grab you a few snacks to tide you over." She pointed the way.

Chandra, Faith, and Eloise were already hovered over the pottery items we could pick out to paint while I noticed the mortals had also come to paint.

"Hi," I walked over to Jo Ellen, Tish, and Hazel. "I'm so glad to see you."

"I don't know how long we will be staying." Tish sounded flustered. "Jo Ellen won't keep her hands off anything."

"Where is your kitty?" Jo Ellen asked with her big eyes wide open.

"I'm telling you that you need to get that girl a kitten." Hazel chirped up before she moseyed on over to the snack table.

"Mrs. Jones sure is nosy." Tish shook her head and reached over to move Jo Ellen's hand off of a ceramic mug. "You should see her in the neighborhood. Have you seen the show *Bewitched* or are you too young for that?"

"Oh, I know it." I grinned, I knew it in real life as well, but I kept that comment to myself.

"Remember her neighbor Mrs. Kravitz?" she asked and pointed over to Hazel. We both laughed.

"Well, I guess you could have worse neighbors." I glanced out the window and saw Petunia and Oscar standing on the sidewalk along with Violet and Gene.

My heart flip-flopped as I saw Petunia hand baby Orin over to Oscar, strapping him on Oscar's chest and Violet pushing Gene toward him as well.

"Jo Ellen," I bent down, "would you like to go outside with Oscar and maybe help him out with baby Orin?"

"Can I Mommy?" Jo bounced on the balls of her feet. "Plllllleeeeease?" Her body swayed back and forth with her hands clasped behind her back.

"Sure," Tish said with a giggle.

I reached for her hand and we trotted outside along with Mr. Prince Charming.

"How on Earth did I get wrangled into this?" Oscar asked. Fear in his eyes.

"Oh, you look like a pro." I had to swallow the lump that'd formed in my throat. If I hadn't, I might've started to cry because Oscar looked so cute and I suddenly imagined him as a father. Something I'd yet to do.

"I'm not." He patted baby Orin on the hiney.

"Well, I bet you guys can go grab a treat from Wicked Good and if you are very good, I would bet that Oscar will walk you down to look at the kittens in the window of the pet shop." My voice escalated to get them excited.

"Can we?" Gene and Jo Ellen asked at the same time.

"You are going to pay," Oscar warned me.

"Promise?" I winked and kissed him before he shot out after the kids who'd already run across the street and into Wicked Good. That included Mr. Prince Charming too.

I stood there for a moment and watched as Oscar gathered them up and let them look at all the treats.

"Cute right?" Eloise joined me. "You two are going to make me the cutest grand-nephew and niece."

"Both?" I asked with a nervous laugh.

"We shall see." She grinned.

"I'm so glad you are here." I tucked my arm in hers as we turned back around to make it back inside the craft shop. "I need to go visit a village in Ohio and Oscar doesn't want me to go by myself."

"You want me to go?" she asked and answered before I could answer. "I'd love to get away for a day. In fact, I might know some people I can visit while I'm there."

"Great. I can't go tomorrow, because I have some things to do," I knew I wanted to go visit Patch and maybe have some of that tea Hazel Jones had offered me. If what Tish had said about Hazel's nosy side was true, maybe she had seen something. "But what about the day after?"

"I'll meet you at the sprinkle before dawn." She patted my hand as we walked over to the snack table.

I filled my plate with some fruit, chocolates and a couple of finger sandwiches and mentally set my internal clock to meet her about fifteen minutes before the sun started to pop up.

"Is your husband going to kill us?" Tish asked as she, Violet and Petunia huddled near the window as they watched their children.

"No, but you might kill him after he shows them all of those cute kittens Petunia has in her shop window," I said and popped a piece of fruit in my mouth.

"Aren't they adorable?" Petunia gushed.

"Oh no," Tish grumbled. "Jo Ellen has been driving me crazy about a cat ever since the pumpkin patch. I told her that not all cats acted like yours."

"But these kittens are perfect." Petunia pulled Tish aside and gave her the sales pitch about the kittens, leaving me with Violet.

"Is Gene excited about school?" I asked.

"Not really." There was sadness in her voice. "He, or me, isn't sure about the whole boarding school thing."

"He will love it." I took a bite of the sandwich. "My aunt is the dean and I went there. It's safe and fun."

"He's never been away from me. Since birth, he's lived on Tulip Island." She looked out the window. Pride showed on her face as she watched Gene in the window of Wicked Good talking to Oscar.

"Have you heard from your father?" I asked about Victor Draper, the owner of Tulip Island. "And how's Peter doing?"

"Peter," she *tsked*. "He loves the island. Dad's been so busy since it's fall in the states. All the mortals want to do is get away from the cold. But Gene worries me. I feel like he needs something."

"He needs a happy mom." I patted her on the back. "You are just getting your feet wet in this crazy mortal world. Trying to use your spiritual gift for the first time. A new business owner and all while trying to give your son the best life." I glanced out the window to see what she was smiling at.

Oscar had let Gene hold his wand. Since Gene didn't have the special powers yet, he could wave it around without any spells accidently coming out.

"He will learn to use that wand and become a great member of our heritage." I wasn't sure what he'd become or even if he did have powers since he was part mortal from his father and part spiritualist from her, but my intuition did tell me that she needed to spread her wings. "While he is at school, you can test out the waters on your life. Grow your business." I put my arm around her. "Grow friendship." I squeezed. "Romance."

That seemed to brighten her eyes.

"And you can visit Hidden Halls anytime you want. In fact, I'll take you and him on his first day. Walk you around. Introduce you to people." I knew that she was happy with what I was saying. It put her at ease.

Slowly she began to nod her head in agreement.

"Thank you, June." She hugged me. "You are a true friend."

I hugged back, only thoughts of my friend Ophelia popped into my head. I thought she was a true friend too.

"Okay, y'all! Listen up." Leah tucked a piece of her long brown hair behind her ear. "Have you picked out what you want to paint?"

My questions about Violet and Patch were going to have to wait.

"Take your pottery over to a table and sit down. You will find a sponge, bowl of water, a couple of different paint brushes with different sized tips, paints and some rags." She held up each item as she spoke. "You can paint your pottery however you want. If you don't like a color, you can dip your sponge in the water and it will come right off."

We all watched as she made a big blue streak down a pumpkin and wiped it clean.

"I'll be walking around and checking things out." She rocked back and forth on her cowboy boots. "If y'all have a question or need anything, give me a holler."

There was a space between Petunia and Violet. I figured I'd sit there and see if Petunia offered up anything about the meeting with the developer.

I glanced around the room. Tish was seated next to Hazel and helping her with her piece of pottery which was a teapot, perfect for Hazel. Tish caught me looking at her and rolled her eyes.

It brought back memories of me growing up in Locust Grove. Being around those two made me feel more at home than in a spiritual community. I could see Petunia and the Order of Elders had done the right thing by opening up our community, even if it might bring some crime.

There wasn't a city or town out there that didn't have some sort of criminal activity, only ours happened to be a murder at the moment.

Chandra had picked out a piece of pottery in the shape of a star. She had already painted the entire thing blue like the blue stars painted on her fingernails.

Eloise had picked a ceramic sign that she could use in her garden where she grew the incense and herbs she needed for her morning smudge.

Petunia had changed her mind from a cat to a birdhouse with pumpkins and vines along the bottom, while I picked the cat with a witch's hat perched on his head.

Of course I painted the cat white with a black hat. It was going to make the perfect addition to A Charming Cure.

Everyone seemed to have a great time as the hours flew by. Leah had promised our pottery would be dried and sealed before the All Hallows' Eve celebration and Tish and Hazel could pick theirs up tomorrow.

I made a mental note to pick them up for them. It gave me a good reason to stop by Hazel's and pick her brain.

Oscar and the kids were still down at Glorybee Pet Shop. Tish had promised Petunia she'd think about it. I'd already thought about it. I'd grab the white kitten on my way to see them along with the pottery, that way she couldn't say no.

"I'm beat." Oscar fell down on the couch as soon as we got home.

I hung my cloak up next to the door and put my purse on the counter. Mr. Prince Charming jumped up on the back of the couch and made himself comfortable for the night.

"Who knew kids could be so exhausting?" Oscar looked over at me. "Do you think we were that rambunctious?"

"We probably didn't know if we were or not because we relied on each other." I grabbed the chilled wine out of the refrigerator and two wineglasses and walked over to him. I set the bottle and glasses on the coffee table and sat on the edge of the couch.

Oscar sat up and worked his magic on my shoulders as he kneaded away my stress of the day. I should've given him a back rub instead, but it felt too good.

I tucked my chin to my chest and let him rub, push, and rub some more before I uncorked the bottle and poured two large glasses.

"Long day?" I asked when I noticed the exhaustion set in his blue eyes.

"Yeah." He took the glass and eased back on the couch. I joined him. "I went by Broussert's office today. He was out but his secretary let me take a look at his schedule."

"Anything?" I asked and twisted my body to the side with my leg tucked in a V, facing him. I took a sip of my wine and listened.

"He has been out of town for the past couple of weeks on vacation with his wife. I even checked with the resort and they have him there on the night and morning of Patty's death, so that rules him out." Oscar rubbed his temples. "As much as I want to believe Colton, I just can't shake the hatred he has for the guy. He just keeps saying that he's an enemy and they didn't see eye-to-eye."

I looked off into the distance and thought about what Oscar was telling me.

"I have a surprise." Oscar sat up and put his glass on the table. He got up and walked out the front door only to reappear with a big pumpkin. He set it on the kitchen table.

My heart warmed. He remembered.

"I love you." I hurried over to him and threw my arms around him. "Every year since we were ten."

"It's a tradition. Our tradition." His lips met mine. "I hope as we get older, we have many more traditions that include kids."

"Kids?" I pulled away. As much as I loved seeing him with Gene, Jo, and Orin, the thought of me being responsible for a small person sort of scared me.

I walked over to the kitchen and pulled out the pumpkin carving kit from underneath the sink. Oscar had already grabbed a knife and started to cut the lid on the top of the pumpkin.

"Yeah," his smile weakened my knees. "You do want a little June, right?" He tugged the seed-dripping lid off the pumpkin.

"Maybe I want a little Oscar." I carefully used my fingers to rake the seeds out. Seeds were good for potions and for roasting. "But I'm not sure about my ability to be a mother. I mean, Darla was wonderful and I truly thank her for policing everything I did and ate, but I'm not so sure I'd do that with my child. Our child."

The words left my mouth leaving me with a fear that I'd never known. A fear that I was sure was only maternal.

"June," Oscar set the knife down and placed his hands on each of my shoulders. He turned me toward him. His big blue eyes staring down into my soul as though he could read and see every fear that was bubbling deep within me. "We will be wonderful parents. The kind of parents that we really wished we had. You had a wonderful mom. I didn't have any parents. We will make it a family that suits us. Good food. Bad food. Fights. Good times and all." He looked at the pumpkin and then back at me.

He bent down and kissed both sides of my neck and finally finding my lips.

"Maybe we should start practicing the art of having children before we actually do." Oscar's words warmed my body. "This pumpkin can wait."

"Sounds good," I mumbled, letting my body melt into his arms.

Chapter Fifteen

The next morning I'd gotten up early to find that Oscar had already left. He left a scribbled note on his pillow that he'd had an idea and wanted to check it out and he'd call me later.

He was so intent on saving Colton, he was grabbing at straws. I wasn't sure if my promise to Ophelia was getting in the way of his investigation.

I rolled over and looked at Madame Torres. She'd been awfully quiet this whole time. I rubbed my hand over the top of her glass ball. Her insides swirled and twirled popping little images like the pottery, kitten, and roses, reminding me of my itinerary. The last thing she showed me was the leaf charm.

I grabbed the charm bracelet I'd taken off and laid next to her before Oscar and I had gone to bed and clasped it on.

"Where are you, Mr. Prince Charming?" I threw the covers off and sat up in the bed looking around the room.

I padded down the hall and into the kitchen where there was a cup next to the coffee pot that Oscar had put there for me. A smile curled in my heart as I filled the cup and looked out over Whispering Falls.

"Patch," I reminded myself that I wanted to stop by and see him as well, but found it odd that Madame Torres hadn't reminded me of that.

The clinking sound of chains echoed up the hill and I watched as Eloise eased down the main street, tossing the incense side-to-side and up and down. Mr. Prince Charming trotted alongside her. He must've gone out with Oscar.

I quickly took a shower and dressed in a pair of black skinny pants and a black turtleneck sweater. The sky was grey. I could see Eloise's breath as she chanted, which told me it was colder than yesterday.

The half-carved pumpkin was sitting on the table. I dragged my hand over it and giggled. Being married was more than I had ever dreamed. Being married to Oscar was the magical dream come true. I grabbed a handful of pumpkin seeds and put them in a baggie.

A faint light streamed down the hall from the bedroom. I walked back to find Madame Torres awake.

"Who is it you seek or shall I ask who is it that seeks you?" Her head bobbled up and down in the water. The yellow turban wobbled back and forth on her head. The black lining and yellow makeup was bold along her eyes along with the bright red lipstick painted across her lips.

"I hope no one is seeking me." I picked up and looked into my crystal ball familiar. "I'm not having nightmares, so I don't think that I'm in immediate danger."

"Alise Lance seeeeeeeeeks," her words moved with the waves, "youuuuuuu." She went black.

"What does that mean?" I shook the ball and nothing but pumpkins and orange glitter floated around. "Madame Torres? I'm going to see her tomorrow."

Nothing. I growled and decided to take her along with me.

I stuck her in the bottom of my bag and strapped it across me before I grabbed the baggie full of pumpkin seeds and threw my cloak around my shoulders.

A breeze that knifed lungs and tingled bare skin flew up under my cloak as I scurried down the hill knowing I'd find solace inside A Charming Cure.

I reached in my bag and pulled out the pumpkin seeds and my key to the door. I wasn't sure what I was going to use the pumpkin seeds for but my intuition told me to grab them this morning.

"June!" Violet called from the sidewalk. She was standing down the street in front of Magical Moments. "Can I talk to you for a minute?"

"Sure." I waved her to come in my shop and pushed the old skeleton key into the lock, twisting it to open. I felt something run across the toe of my boot. I flipped on the light and Mr. Prince Charming sat in the middle of the store dragging his long white tail across the floor.

Mewl. He purred, greeting me.

"Just where have you been?" My brows lifted and I picked him up, taking him to the back of the shop, and placed him on the stool. "You and Oscar left me this morning," I dug into my bag, "alone with her." I put Madame Torres on the counter.

"Oh thanks," Madame Torres's sarcastic tone billowed out.

The bell over the door dinged and Violet walked in.

"Do you mind flipping on the cauldron crock-pot?" I pointed to the table next to the door. "I forgot."

While she did that, I disappeared behind the partition and flipped on the cauldron. There was plenty of time to work the pumpkin seeds into a potion before the shop opened and I was curious to see what the plan was in my magical world.

"I've been thinking about what you said last night." She walked up to the counter and ran her hand down Mr. Prince Charming. He purred in delight. He wrapped his tail around her wrist.

Oh no, I grimaced. There were a lot of things I'd said last night.

"You know, when you offered to take me and Gene to Hidden Halls." She forced a smile across her face. "I. . ." she gulped. "I've met someone."

My head jerked her way. Now we were getting to the juicy stuff.

"And as much as I do want Gene here and involved, I also want to pursue the relationship and see if it goes anywhere. I know Gene will have so much more fun at Hidden Halls instead of here and I know I'll have more time to explore my love life, but I . . .I . . . ."

The pumpkin seeds in my grip were heating up. The seeds had to be for her, but legally I couldn't read another spiritualist or give them a potion. It was against the by-laws.

"We are friends." Her eyes dipped.

"We are friends." I curled a fist around the seeds. "And I am more than happy to help a friend in need because we were friends before I even knew you were one of us." I winked, knowing I was using semantics to get away with my plan to help Violet. "How about if we go visit Hidden Halls not tomorrow but the next day?"

"That's the first day of the All Hallows' Eve festivities," she reminded me.

"That's right." I shook my head. "What am I thinking? But," I shrugged, "I could go early that morning and Faith can open for me if you can swing it."

"I can swing it." She looked over her shoulder when Faith walked in the door. "Hi." The two greeted each other. Violet looked back at me, "Don't tell anyone about my possible love interest."

Faith was stocking the goodie table with more delicious treats from Wicked Good.

"I've got to go make some deliveries," Faith called from the door. I could see the Wicked Good cupcake car parked in front of the shop through the display window. "But I'll be back because the breeze told me you need me today."

"I do. But take your time." I waved 'bye to her and turned back to Violet. "Spill." I encouraged her to tell me about the gossip I'd already heard.

"I don't have time now, but I'll see you in a couple of days." She bounced on her toes, twirled around and headed to the door.

"Do you mind turning the sign?" I pointed to the closed sign on the door. "I know it's early, but there might be some early birds."

My head slightly tilted, my eyes lowered as I watched her traipse down the front steps of the shop. There was nothing more exciting than seeing someone falling in love. I opened my palm and looked at the bag full of pumpkin seeds.

"Someone is in need of a little romance." I dragged my hand over Mr. Prince Charming when I walked past him. "And I have just the plan."

I knew I could make a delicious pumpkin spice coffee creamer that would send Violet and Patch into love overload. It would probably be good for Patch. There was nothing better than love to help heartache. Even though I knew he'd never feel the same since losing his twin, I also knew loving and being loved by someone did help fill some of the void.

The cauldron had already started to bubble a frothy orange. I dropped in the seeds and watched as the mixture turned to a translucent tonic. My intuition told me to add some tonka beans. My hand slid down the shelf of ingredients and stopped once I reached the empty bottle.

I plucked it off the shelf and grinned. Before Happy Herb opened, I'd have had to wait for KJ.

"Let's go," I said to Mr. Prince Charming and grabbed my bag and cloak.

I quickly locked the shop door behind me and rushed down the street hoping KJ was already in his shop preparing for the morning.

I knocked on the door before I turned the handle to push it open.

"Hello?" I stuck my head in and called out.

"I've been waiting for you." KJ stood at the counter in his new mortal street clothes. "I'm told you are needing tonka beans."

He shook a new bottle of the magical seeds up in the air.

"Love or money?" he asked.

"Love." I grinned and walked across the amazing floor. "And I love that you are here."

"I bet you do." His dark eyes appraised me. "June," his voice lowered, "is this for a mortal?"

"Don't make me tell you." Worry swept across my face as my brows furrowed. "Or make me lie."

"Oh, June Heal." He *tsked.* "Will you ever learn?"

"Probably not." I quipped, "And that is what you love about me."

He lowered his arm and extended the bottle for me to take.

"You know that love always rules and that true love will find its home in its own time no matter how much we try to help it along with our special touch," he warned.

"A little nudge won't hurt." I held the bottle close. "You stay warm!" I called and walked out the door just in time to see Petunia opening her shop and Mr. Prince Charming darting inside.

When she flipped on the light, I saw the little kittens pop up. I couldn't wait to take the runt to Jo Ellen today, which meant I had to hurry and get the potion made and the shop in order for Faith to take charge.

"Did Violet spill the beans on her and Patch?" That was the first question out of Faith's mouth when she came back to relieve me so I could run through my daily sleuthing chores.

"She did not." I shook my head. "You are a busy-body."

"I'm a young girl who is a sucker for love." She twirled barely missing knocking over a customer. "Oops." She giggled.

"Everything is ready for you. I've stocked all the shelves. We've been crazy busy. Everyone is excited about the celebration." I grabbed my cloak. "I've got to stop in Locust Grove and get some candy for the kids for All Hallows' Eve—do you want me to grab some for you?"

"Oh, that'd be great." Faith leaned over the counter. "Raven had asked me to get some while I was at the Piggly Wiggly when I dropped off the Wicked Good pastries, but I completely spaced out. I was going to do it in the morning, but you would save me a trip."

"You can't do it in the morning, you already promised me you'd open the shop," I reminded her.

"That's right." She sucked in a deep breath.

"Are you sure you can handle today and tomorrow?" I asked, a little concerned about her behavior. She was young, but not forgetful. I'd never seen her so scatter-brained.

"I don't know," she whispered and motioned for me to come behind the partition away from customers' ears. "The breeze has been sketchy."

"What do you mean?" I asked, my intuition flipped on. It curled from my toes into my stomach up into my throat.

"Things are happening too fast for Whispering Falls and the breeze is getting confused. The voodoo doll. The breeze said that the voodoo doll was amateurish." She was on autopilot, tuned into her spiritual gift. "There is love, deception, and people aren't who you think they are. The breeze circles around and around as if it's not sure which way it will go." Her empty eyes stared right through me. "It whips one direction only to circle around. It's a never-ending cycle and there is no clear ending."

Her head fell forward. Her shoulders slumped.

I put my hand on her. "Faith? Are you okay?"

Her shoulders heaved up and down as she sucked to get in air. I grabbed the stool and dragged it behind the partition, forcing her to sit down.

"Go." Slowly her chin lifted. "You must go and find the killer."

I didn't wait any longer. Things were worse than I thought. I grabbed a handful of June's Gems off the snack table and threw them in the bottom of my bag before I walked out the door.

A fierce, steady wind shrilled down the main street. I brought my hand up to my mouth and took a deep bite into my chocolaty treat hoping the stress I was feeling would just go away.

Chapter Sixteen

"It's as cold as a room full of ex-wives." Leah cackled when I walked in. "My daddy used to say that."

"Your daddy must be quite a character." I quickly shut the door behind me.

"Your cat ain't ready quite yet." She walked over to the table of pottery we'd painted last night and checked the cat with the hat that I'd made.

"I'm heading over to Tish Chapman's house to take her daughter a kitten from Glorybee and I thought I'd stop by and grab her and Hazel Jones's pottery so they didn't have to make a trip out on this cold day," I said, even though my intentions weren't as true as they sounded.

I did want to make sure the runt kitten went to a good home and I knew in my gut that it belonged to Jo Ellen and I also knew that runts generally didn't find homes, though Petunia would keep it if not. Plus, I really wanted to see if Hazel had seen or heard anything since she lived so close to Patch. Then I suddenly wondered if Oscar had questioned Patch's whereabouts the night his brother was murdered. After all, I did hear them fighting.

"You are so nice. I swear. I love living here." Leah walked to the back of her shop and pulled out some white tissue paper and a couple green bags with a white chevron design. She curled their items in the paper and I walked around looking at all the items she had for sale in her shop.

"Did you make all of this?" I noticed the pretty glass bead necklaces and matching bracelets.

"Mmhmm. It helps with stress, you know?" She walked over and handed me the bags.

"I know all about stress." I took a bag in each hand. "Thanks so much. Now I've got to get that kitten."

"I'm giving a beading class in the winter if you want to sign up. It's not like last night, a one time deal. It's actually a class where we will make some jewelry pieces and learn techniques. So it's a few weeks long." She handed me a flyer with the dates and times. "I figured it was probably slow around here in the winter and it will bring in some business."

"I'll definitely do it." I was happy to see the times were at night. "I'll be sure to have some of the other gals sign up too. A weekly girls' night."

"Yay!" She clapped and bounced on the balls of her feet. "You stay warm out there." She shut the door behind me when I walked out.

The weather didn't deter any tourists. The street was filled with shoppers and smiling faces which made life so much easier. And seeing those kittens in the window made me joyful. They were so cute as they jumped and rolled on top of each other. The white kitten was off by itself.

I hurried inside. Mr. Prince Charming was sitting on the live tree planted in the back corner of the shop next to a hedgehog and squirrel. It looked as if they were eating something. His tail dangled down and swept to and fro.

Petunia was helping out a customer in the lizard section of the shop. I helped myself to the window where the kittens were. They all ran over to me and meowed, batting at me wanting any attention they could get. The little white kitten stayed in the corner. Its big green eyes looking at me. I put my hands out in front of me and motioned for it to come.

The other kittens parted and the little white kitten trotted over. I picked it up and its light purr was music to my ears.

"You are going to love where you are going." I snugged the kitten up to my face and loved on it. The other kittens didn't seem to mind as they continued to tumble and pounce on each other.

"For Jo Ellen?" Petunia walked up. There was a lizard perched on her shoulder.

"It is. I hope they take it." I held the cute kitten up to my face and looked into its precious eyes.

Petunia took the lizard off of her shoulder and held it in her hand. She dragged her finger down its bony spine.

"It's going to take a little coaxing, but put it down as Tish protests and the magic will happen all on its own." Petunia pushed the lizard into her messy up-do. She curled her free hand around my elbow. "Now, let's talk about you."

"What about me?" I asked, an uneasy feeling sweeping over me.

"Oscar. Orin. Jo. Gene." Her words were static. "I don't think I need to say any more."

"Let us be honeymooners first." I cuddled the kitten up to my heart to shield any vibes that might be electrifying out of my body.

"Looking back, if I'd known the joy that Orin gives me and Gerald, I'd have started earlier." Petunia and Gerald were both older spiritualists. Gerald had already been married, had Arabella, owner of Magical Moments, and divorced before he'd met and married Petunia.

Most of us figured she was going to be the old spiritualist single cat lady. Now she was not.

"You are a great mom. But tell me about the fight between Patch and Mr. Broussert." I slipped it in hoping she'd just go with it.

"That was a mess." She glanced around the shop. Everyone seemed to be happy. Who couldn't be happy surrounded by a shop full of amazing animals. "He is paying Patch a lot of money to be the farmer and Patch refused to live on the farm in the farm house."

"Do you know why?" I asked.

"He said that he wanted to be in the Whispering Falls section since his business was there. Something about paying two different taxes." She rolled her eyes. "We don't pay taxes. Yet."

Which we didn't. The Order of Elders had made sure it looked as if we did.

"What do you mean?" I questioned. "Gosh," I bit my lip. "It seems like we missed a lot while we were gone on our honeymoon."

"Speaking of Broussert, he really isn't such a great guy and I do wish he didn't have an alibi for the night of Patty's murder because I could see him doing something so awful." She let go of my arm and drew her hands to her chest. "He insisted that he get something out of the development deal between us and Locust Grove. It was proposed that the money made from the sale of the agri-hood farm and us purchasing items from there would be enough." Her lashes drew down her cheeks, leaving a shadow. "I got word late last night that he wants to own a building or shop here."

"A new shop?" I wondered how that was going to work with our magic.

"No. The Crazy Crafty Chick shop. His wife loves to do crafts and she came to see the shop yesterday and loved it. He wants to own the building which would make Leah have to rent it from him." She sucked in a deep inhale and held it.

"How on Earth would that work with our," I twiddled my fingers in the air.

She did a simple shrug before she was called over to help a customer.

I glanced up at Mr. Prince Charming. He looked at me and jumped down off the limb. He put his front paws on the trunk of the tree and did a long stretch before he started to sharpen his claws on the tree. He darted over to me.

"You ready?" I asked.

Mewl, he darted to the door and waited for me.

"June," Petunia called across the shop. "Grab that bag next to the door. It's for Tish and Jo's new kitten."

"Thanks!" I grabbed the bag and opened the door. Mr. Prince Charming ran out. "Wait," I turned back to Petunia but she'd already started to help another customer. "His wife was there yesterday? But I thought they were on vacation?" I whispered to myself and stepped out into the grey day.

No matter how many layers I had on to ward off the cold, it still wasn't enough to shoo away the chill in my bones.

Chapter Seventeen

I tried to call Oscar a couple of times on my way back up to the cottage. I wanted to ask him if he was certain that Broussert was on a family vacation because that didn't add up to what Petunia had said about his wife, but he didn't answer.

There was something off about that entire situation and I couldn't help but wonder if it had anything to do with Patty's death, especially if Broussert had mistaken him for Patch.

The Green Machine rattled into the new neighborhood. It dawned on me that I'd yet to figure out which house was Tish and Jo Ellen's, but when I saw them walking down the sidewalk, I pulled to the side.

"Hey, strangers." I waved out the window after I rolled it down.

"Hi, June!" Jo Ellen waved with an over eager enthusiasm.

"Hi, June," Tish wasn't as excited as Jo, but I was greeted with a smile. "We are out for a brisk walk. I think Jo had too much candy apple the other night and her tummy is still upset. That's why I'm home from work."

"Yeah. My belly hurts." Jo rubbed her stomach. "Mommy said fresh air was all I needed, but it's not helping."

"Maybe this will help?" I picked the little kitten off my lap and held her up.

"Oh, Mommy!" Jo squealed and tugged on her mom.

Tish gave me a sideways glance. "I don't know."

"Where do you live so I can park?" I noticed a car coming down the street and I didn't want to endanger Jo or block the road.

"We live right next to Hazel." She pointed to a modest house.

"You mean Hazel is sandwiched between you and Patch?" I shook my head knowing Hazel was a busy lady if she was as nosy as I'd heard.

"Yes." Tish nodded.

"Can I hold the kitty?" Jo asked.

"When we get home." Tish responded and I slowly drove down the street and parked in their driveway. I strapped my bag across my body.

Jo had almost beaten me to her house before I could even get my door open. She stretched out her arms for the kitten and once it was securely in her arms, ran inside her house.

"June, you are awfully sweet," Tish said when I gave her the Crazy Crafty Chick's package. "But I honestly don't know if I can take care of a kitten. I'm a single mom and I have to work. I barely have time for myself after I get all of Jo's needs taken care of."

"Cats aren't any trouble." I pointed over to my ornery fairy-god cat. He didn't seem to even know we'd made it to our destination as he snoozed in the corner of the dashboard on the passenger side. "They only want you to feed them and clean their litter box."

I grabbed the bag off the floorboard that Petunia had given me.

"Here are all the supplies you are going to need for a long time. Courtesy of Petunia." I handed it to her.

"I can't say no." Tish's words were very welcoming. "Look at her."

Both of us looked at her house. Through the front window you could see Jo playing with the kitten. It was a far sight from the scared kitten in the corner of the Glorybee display window.

"Match made in heaven." I grinned.

"Mmhhhmmm," Tish hummed. She let out a sudden gasp. Her eyes weren't on Jo and the kitten. They were on Patch Potter who was driving a tractor down the street toward the farm.

Oh no, my intuition groaned.

"Are you okay?" I asked because she had a surprised look on her face.

"I'm fine. I guess Patch caught me off guard." She faked a smile.

"I know. I feel so bad about his brother. I don't have siblings, but I could only imagine how hard it'd be knowing someone murdered them." I watched as Patch's tractor disappeared around the corner.

"What happened?" she asked.

"Patch's twin brother, Patty, was found murdered in the pumpkin patch a couple of nights ago." I honestly figured she knew something because the chemistry that set my intuition off when she looked at him, told me there was definitely something between them.

"I had no idea." She put her hand to her face. "No wonder," she dragged her hands to her lips and her eyes to the ground.

"No wonder what?" I asked.

"Y'all want some afternoon tea?" Hazel broke over our conversation.

"I wish I could, but I have to go inside and take care of my new cat June gave us." Tish laughed and headed on inside her house.

Darn. That was a very interesting conversation and Tish was definitely in shock. Maybe Hazel could shed some light on what was going on around here. In fact, I was counting on it.

"I can." I reached inside of the Green Machine and pulled her bag out. The timing couldn't have been any more perfect. "And I have your teapot you painted last night. Say, how is your shoulder?"

"You know." She circled it around a few times clockwise and then counter-clockwise. "I don't know what you gave me, but it worked the first night."

"Great. Keep using it until it's all gone," I instructed her. "Then you go back to your doctor and let me know what he says."

"I will." She grabbed the bag from me.

Mr. Prince Charming stood up on the dash and curled his back into a big stretch and let out a yawn then jumped out of the car before I shut the door. He sat down next to me and pulled up a front paw, licking it.

Hazel opened the bag and pulled out the beautiful teapot.

"That was fast." She eyed the teapot and then me. "I thought I heard her say it'd be ready today, but. . ." she tapped at her ear. "The old hearing ain't what it used to be. She must have a really fast kiln. I don't much about glazing, but she sure did do a fine job."

I just smiled. I knew that Leah had to have used a little bit of her magic to get the mortal's project finished.

"What about that?" I asked and briskly rubbed my hands together.

"Oh, yes." She continued to look at the teapot as we walked up to her house. "You come on too." With the pot still in her grip, she used it to motion for Mr. Prince Charming.

We walked in and I was swept into a sea of orangesickle. If the walls weren't painted peach, they were wallpapered in a peach design. The carpet was cream and the drapes were a cream and peach design.

"Your house makes me hungry for ice cream," I teased and walked into the family room that was in the back of the house.

"Don't you just love it?" She moseyed into the kitchen and we followed her. It too was. . .peach.

"Did you design it?" I asked and helped her retrieve mugs from the cabinet.

She got out creamer from the refrigerator and a jar of honey.

"I didn't. The designers of the agri-hood brought in a fancy interior decorator after I was about to pull out of the development." She held up the creamer. "Creamer? It's from the farm. This too." She held up the honey jar.

"No thank you." I took my mug of tea and pumped the individual steeper up and down, allowing the full flavor of the tea to seep into the hot water. "This is just what I need to get the chill off."

I followed her into the family room and we sat on the couch that overlooked a portion of Patch's pumpkin farm. Mr. Prince Charming paced in front of her back door.

"Does he need to go pee?" she asked.

"No he's fine." I tried to give him a look, but he ignored me. He continued to pace and bat at the door. "He's not used to being cooped up and he likes to roam, so if you ever see him, shoo him back to my shop."

Mr. Prince Charming stopped and looked at me. I swear he gave me an evil eye, but I ignored him.

"This is a beautiful view." I gazed out the window. The pumpkins were bright even with the grey clouds looming. "Why on Earth did you almost pull out of living here?" I asked, wanting to know her answer.

"I'm old. My hearing is not so great and my eyes have cataracts." She took a sip of the steaming tea out of her mug. "I know I'm pretty spry and I don't look that old, but I am."

I tried not to smile too big. She was cute, but I knew she was old.

"The prices of these homes are ridiculous. Broussert had made it sound really good and when I picked out my lot, I thought it was going to be much larger." Her thin brows pointed up. She shook her head. "The cost of the monthly HOA fee is more than most people's mortgage." She *tsked.*

I couldn't help but notice Hazel's framed photos on the wall of a man that looked similar to her. I stood up and walked over to the windows.

"You still have an amazing view and no one can build behind you. Plus, you are in the Whispering Falls village not Locust Grove." That had to be a perk.

"That's weird too. Now I know you live there, but I just think it's strange that after all this time, your village hasn't had a mayor, or any sort of real laws. But I hear all that's changing." She took a sip.

"You know that I'm married to Oscar who does work in both Locust Grove Sheriff's department as well as Whispering Falls Police Department. I grew up in Locust Grove." I wanted to put her mind at ease. I was worried that this would be the case with most mortals. "We didn't need to have our own laws since we were under the umbrella of Locust Grove. It's kinda like county versus city laws."

In the state of Kentucky, a county can be made up of several small cities with different laws and departments in each. It was a great excuse to give her and not let her on to just how special Whispering Falls was.

She nodded her head. Mr. Prince Charming had finally settled down and just sat at the door looking out.

"Is this your son?" I walked in front of the photo.

"Ummmhmmm," she nodded her head. "He's so handsome. He thought moving here was going to be a wonderful idea. That's my daughter-in-law and grandson. I'm hoping you will get to meet them at the All Hallows' Eve celebration. My grandson is going to be dressed as a pirate this year."

"Oh." Joy bubbled up inside of me. "I love that."

Hearing that Hazel was going to embrace our village as an active citizen and all it had to offer really did put warmth in my heart.

A few seconds later, a movement from outside caught my attention. Patch had parked the tractor in his back yard and was walking toward the pumpkin farm.

"Poor Patch." I frowned and turned back around. "I feel so bad for him."

"Why?" Hazel asked.

"You didn't hear?" I asked.

"His brother was found dead in his pumpkin farm a couple nights ago." I guessed the mortal community wasn't as aware as our spiritual community. "His twin brother."

"Oh no." Hazel's face swept with a look of concern. "Do they know who did it?"

"Not yet, but Oscar has a few leads." I walked back over and sat down. "You didn't happen to see any strange activity did you?" I asked, baiting her for some gossip that we might find useful in helping us solve the crime.

She shook her head and pursed her wrinkly lips like she was doing some hard thinking.

"Well." She looked around the room like someone was going to hear her. "Tish next door is a nice woman, she really is and that daughter of hers. Don't get me started on how adorable she is, but..." She sat up on the edge of her seat with her tea cradled in her hands. I noticed a couple of scratches on them. "I have seen her over there." She jerked her head toward Patch's house. "I didn't know Patch had a brother, so maybe she was fussing with him."

"Fussing?" I asked.

"Mmmhmmm." She nodded her head and brought the mug to her lips, taking another sip. "That's some good tea."

"It is. But what were you saying about Tish and her fussing with Patch?" I steered her back on the right track. Another thing she could add to her list of ailments was forgetfulness. She changed subjects so fast I was having a hard time keeping up.

"Oh yeah." She eased back into her seat. "I was tending my garden when it all took place a few nights ago."

"Like two nights ago?" I asked, wondering if I was going to be able to place Tish at the crime scene, even though I already knew she had taken Jo Ellen to the pumpkin farm.

But did she and Patty have an argument and Hazel thought it was Patch since she didn't know he had a brother? If so, why would Tish want him dead?

Fear knotted in my gut as I recalled Tish watching Patch drive that tractor a little while ago.

"She was saying something about them laying down together. If you know what I mean." Her brows wiggled up and down.

My jaw dropped. Tish and Patch together? In bed? Not only did that give Tish emotional ties to him, but he'd have to explain our world.

"He said something about he was not for her and that she didn't want him in her or Jo Ellen's life." Hazel continued to gossip. And I listened more. "She said that if she could handle being a single parent after an abusive husband, then she definitely could handle whatever it was that he was hiding."

It was so hard for me to fathom why Patch would risk our spiritual world in the first place. I knew that my mom had known, but that was back in the day before technology and the world was just different. We could stay anonymous better. Today people were more observant and didn't mind getting all up in your business.

"She said she'd do anything to keep him." The knock at the door made me jump. Hazel set her tea down. "If you'll excuse me for a minute."

I got up with her.

"We need to get going." Mr. Prince Charming and I followed her.

As I was standing behind her, Hazel opened the door. Tish standing at the door with a knife in her hand was the last thing I remembered before everything went black.

Chapter Eighteen

"Are you sure you're okay?" Tish was sitting next to me on Hazel's couch. Patch was standing over me, and Hazel was back to drinking her tea. "I mean when I came over to give Hazel the knife I'd borrowed to cut Jo's pumpkin, you just went down. Luckily, Patch was walking between the houses from his pumpkin farm and he helped us get you to the couch."

"Hell, you've had it this long, you might as well keep it." Sarcasm was deep rooted in Hazel's voice. "She says she doesn't keep sharp objects in the house. Child proof." Hazel rolled her eyes. "My parents never shielded me from nothing. I didn't my boy either. That's what's wrong with this world."

Tish rolled her eyes back at Hazel. She reached out to me. "Are you sure you are okay?"

"I'm fine." I shoved Mr. Prince Charming off my chest. "I do this when I'm a little stressed."

I gulped trying not to have my game face slip. How long had she had the knife? Long enough to have poked the holes in Patty's side?

Jo Ellen was sitting cross-legged on the floor shaking the shinola out of Madame Torres. "Where did the lady go? Here lady?" She held it in her little hands and shook poor Madame Torres.

"I'll take that." I tried to reach out and pulled my hand back over my mouth. I felt a little nauseous.

"It fell out of your bag and it's keeping her quiet. While you were passed out, she said some lady spooked her. Such an imagination," Tish said. "You have so many unique things, June." Tish's eyebrows drew together. "Are you okay? Are you going to be sick?"

"I'm fine. Just stressed." My guts were in a knot over Madame Torres. She was already a crabby crystal ball; this was going to throw her over the edge.

"Or pregnant," Hazel chirped.

"Pregnant?" Silly notion. "I'm not pregnant."

At least I didn't think I was pregnant. Oh gosh. I hoped I wasn't pregnant.

"Stay down and let me get you something to drink." Patch put his hand on my shoulder when I tried to sit up.

"Diet Coke would be good." My mouth was dry and a soda sounded good for some reason.

"Mmmhmmm, cravings," Hazel murmured.

"I have some at my house. I'll get it because I need to check on the kitten." Tish put her hand on top of Patch's. The electricity between the two of them was almost unbearable. "You sit here. Come on Jo Ellen. Put the snow globe back in June's bag and give it to her."

Jo Ellen did what her mom told her to do and Hazel walked them to the front door.

"Are you sure you are okay?" Patch asked. "I can call Oscar if we need to."

I knew Patch was asking the underlying question if this was witch related.

"I'm fine. I do this when I'm stressed." I pushed his hand away when he tried to stop me from sitting up again. "Say, why don't your neighbors know that you had a brother? A twin?"

"He wasn't staying and there was no sense in making up some story about where we are from and ever risk them finding out that we are strictly a witch community. Too much risk." He leaned on his thighs with his forearms, his hands clasped between his legs. "I'm just not sure I'm going to be able to stay here and do this."

"You are." I didn't know why I was encouraging him to stay when I thought he could be the killer, but my intuition took over and the words dribbled out of my mouth. "You are a good farmer. It takes time to blend in with the rest of the world. Do you think that Patty wasn't able to do that and someone killed him? Or maybe someone had mistaken him for you?"

Thoughts of him breaking Tish's heart swirled into my head. Love was always a perfect motive to kill someone.

"Your husband asked me all of these questions." Patch stood up when the front door opened.

"Are you dating anyone that would make someone a little jealous?" I asked right as Tish walked in.

Abruptly she stopped and looked at Patch as if she were waiting for his answer. He looked at her. The electricity between them had iced. He slid his eyes back to me and shook his head.

Tish dropped the glass of Diet Coke on Hazel's carpet.

"Good gravy!" Hazel jumped up. "Y'all get on out of my house!" She jutted her finger toward the door. "You've caused enough problems around here!"

"But." I wanted to ask Hazel what she meant by that. "I just want to ask you a question," I stammered as she pushed on my back to shove me out the door.

Patch and Tish didn't need to be told again. They both hurried out and took off in the directions of their respective houses.

"I'm done here. Goodbye." With one good shove, Hazel pushed me right on out of her house. I had to give it to the old broad. She was small and mighty.

"Crap." I stood on the porch and the cold whipping wind informed me that I'd forgotten my cloak inside Hazel's house.

"You forgot this!" I turned when I heard Hazel's voice, only to be smacked in the face with my cloak and the sound of the slamming door.

Chapter Nineteen

"I'm telling you that Patch and Tish had spent an intimate night together. She's so mad at him." Oscar was on the other end of the phone. "Hazel had invited me in for tea and I was just going to poke around and ask some questions. She said the night of Patty's death, Tish and Patch got into a lover's quarrel."

I gave him a quick run down of the day's activities and how my intuition went nuts.

"No one knew Patch had a brother. Don't you think that's strange that the neighbors had no idea?" The pieces of the puzzle were right in front of me and I couldn't fit them together. I was never any good at puzzles.

"I interviewed Tish and Hazel. Hazel's son and grandchild had come to see her that night, so her alibi checked out and Tish was at the pumpkin patch and then put Jo to bed before she took a phone call from her mom. I checked the phone records and with her mom." Oscar was so good at his job. He was always a step ahead of me.

"Then we are back to square one. But I need you to check on Broussert." I'd almost forgotten to tell him about Broussert and his wife. "Petunia had told me that in the deal with Broussert's, he was now trying to own one of the shops for rent money. He said that his wife came to Crazy Crafty Chick a couple days ago and she wants it, but you said that you checked out his whereabouts and he was on vacation with his family. Did that include his wife?" I asked. "Who told you that he was on vacation with his family?"

"They said it was his wife." Oscar's voice drifted off.

"Who?" I asked.

"I'll check it out." His tone held determination.

"Plus I'm not sure it was one of us that killed Patty. Faith said that the wind has been sketchy." I hesitated because I knew he didn't like getting other spiritualists involved and in this conversation I'd already told him what Petunia had said and not Faith, both he'd have to question on his own. "She said that the wind told her the voodoo was amateurish. No one in our community does voodoo. Though, it could've been someone from the outside, but you said the stab job was an amateur and the voodoo doll was an amateur..." I stopped when I realized I was just babbling at that point.

The silence on the other end of the phone was enough to tell me that he would definitely be checking deeper into what I had said.

"I'm really hoping to get some answers from Alise tomorrow," I said.

"I think you can get good answers from Ophelia, but I'll see what you come up with before I go see her. After you are back and you don't have some answers, I'm going to have to go see her and I'm going to have to arrest Colton for the murder." I could feel the tension in his voice through the phone. "There were prints on the wand that belong to Colton."

"But you said the wand was fake. Why would he have fake wands?" I asked.

"He said that he had gotten them for the window display at Ever After Books and someone must've stolen them. And I also went to see Patch," he said.

"He told me that I was asking him the same questions as my husband." I laughed.

"When did you see him?" Oscar asked.

"He helped Tish carry me to the couch." I pulled my lips together and inwardly groaned, putting the Green Machine in park in front of the cottage.

"June," the warning tone in Oscar's voice wasn't pleasant. "What's going on?"

I put my hand on my stomach. Was I pregnant? Panic spread throughout my body.

"You know," I brushed it off. I pushed my bangs out of my eyes and let my hand linger over my phone. Was I? I felt queasy. "I pass out when stressed and after I saw Tish standing there with a knife, I passed out."

"June," his tension turned to worry. "This is why you need to leave the investigation to me."

"No. I'm fine. I'll get a message from Ophelia when I get back from Ohio." I looked down at my bracelet and fiddled with the leaf charm. Things were definitely about to change.

"I was going to stay in Locust Grove tonight, but if you need me, I'll come home," he suggested.

"No. I'm fine." Mr. Prince Charming jumped on the seat and looked out the passenger window. "I'm home and it's late. I'm sure Faith has closed up shop and she's coming in the morning. I think I'll go spend the night with Eloise since we are leaving early."

"That's a good idea." Even though I couldn't see it, I knew he was smiling.

Oscar loved how close Eloise and I were. Plus, I wanted to pick her brain about the blended marriage like Darla's and my dad's because I still felt haunted by the fact Tish wanted to have a relationship with Patch, even though he'd told her he couldn't. I wondered how long he'd be able to keep the electric currents between them at bay because it didn't take a spiritualist to see they both cared deeply for each other. It made me wonder how Violet would feel about it.

Oscar and I said goodbye and I headed on in the house. Mr. Prince Charming rushed back to the bedroom and headed straight for the closet. He knew exactly where my tapestry overnight bag was and he loved going to see Eloise.

I pulled Madame Torres out of the bottom of my bag and set her on the bedside table. Slowly I ran my hand in a circular motion over her glass globe.

"Don't even think about talking to me for a century," Madame Torres said in a feisty voice.

"A century? I could be dead by then."

"Good," Madame Torres's face floated around the globe. She looked guilty being so mean to me. "Are you pregnant? Because if you are, I'm retiring."

"Why would you say that?" I asked.

"Those wretched people talked about it. Hazel told them that you and Oscar couldn't keep your hands off of each other at the pumpkin farm. It made me mad, so I appeared to the little girl and tried to scare her. She just smiled at me and continued to shake me." Madame Torres's insides swirled in an angry cycle.

I left her alone because when she was angry; the best thing to do was to let her be.

I pulled out my tapestry bag with the leather handles. It was the prettiest bag. I packed a pair of jeans and a heavy sweater, as I wasn't sure what the weather was in Ohio. I was going to ask Madame Torres but that was out of the question. She wasn't going to give me any information right now.

My phone app said it was about the same temp so the few items I packed were perfect and I'd be sure to take my cloak.

The sun had set and the moon seemed bent on hurrying from one dark cloud to another, making me scurry along the woods even faster than normal. The empty autumn tree branches cracked as the howl of the wind took all the silence away. I continued to keep my eyes on Mr. Prince Charming's tail as it wagged in the air and the fireflies dotted my path.

In the distance, the lanterns hanging from the trees that dotted the gravel path alongside Eloise's house that led around to her garden were visible.

"Thank you." I called to the teenagers as they buzzed their way back through the woods and Whispering Falls. "Tell Petunia thank you!"

They darted off and within seconds they were gone.

"Oh I love this time of the year." My heart nearly leapt right out of my chest as I looked over the rows and rows of orange, yellow, red, greens, and deep purple flowers that were all part of Eloise's herb garden.

Her herbs were different from KJ's Happy Herb. Her herbs helped with the cleansing she needed to do as well as her ability to see things in the future.

"I've been expecting you," Eloise called from the garden. "I had to snatch these little buggers before they closed up at midnight." She had a handful of Slippery Sleets in her hand. "You have to cut them between ten p.m. and midnight only on a full moon with the grey cloud salute."

She referred to the moon that'd made it difficult for me to see.

"Let me cut a few more because I want to take them with me tomorrow." She pointed her snipping scissors toward the gazebo that glistened with the twinkling lights there were wrapped around the spindles. "I have a bedtime snack."

I took a quick walk around the garden and stopped next to the dream dust and magic peanuts where there was an abundant amount of Fairy Dust. It would be so awesome if Jo Ellen was a fairy for the All Hallows' Eve celebration and I gave her some real Fairy Dust that would leave a little trail behind her.

"Can I take a bottle of Fairy Dust with me and give it to a little girl in the new agri-hood?" I asked Eloise.

"You know it won't call fairies," she trilled back.

"Just for an effect, not magic." I called and ran my hand across Lucky Clover, but not without making a silent plea to give me luck on helping Oscar solve this crime.

The gazebo was one of my favorite places to sit and enjoy any time of the day. She had a small café table in the middle. Tonight there were four chairs. Sometimes there were more, depending on how many people she'd invited over.

"Who's coming by?" I asked.

"I'm here." Ophelia stepped out of the shadow of the grey cloud just as the moon hopped to the next cloud. "I. . .I wasn't sure where to come because I'd caught Oscar in the driveway across the street from your house in Locust Grove."

"That's where he grew up. He's staying in Locust Grove tonight because he has to work there tonight since he's spending all his days with Colton at the station." There were so many things I wanted to say to her. I took my bag off my shoulder and hung it on the back of the chair. "Have you stopped by to see him?"

"No." If she hadn't shaken her head, I would've had to read her lips, her voice was so faint. "I'm ashamed. I know he didn't kill Patty but I have to find out who did first before I can make things right with him. It won't do any good if both of us are in jail."

"Oscar said he's okay. He did say his fingerprints were all over the wands that were stuck in Patty." I pulled the chair out and looked over the array of goodies Eloise had placed on the three-tiered tower in the middle of the table.

The lemon tart was calling my name, or at least my stomach. I put my hand up to my belly. There was a flutter. Was it a flutter of nerves? Or was it a baby?

"Are you okay?" Ophelia asked and sat down on one of the café chairs.

"I'm fine. Long day." I waved her comment off and put the whole baby thing in the back of my head. I filled the rest of my plate with some fruit and didn't even look at the June's Gems. "Who else is coming?"

"I don't think anyone." She shrugged and slumped down. "How was craft night?"

"It was so cool." I gushed on and on. "Leah is so fun. She's a country girl who just loves life. Violet was there as well and I'm not sure but I think she and a mortal who is living next door to Patch Potter are vying for his attention."

"Really? A mortal and a spiritualist. Who will he pick?" That made her eyes light up. "That's so exciting."

"I am having a lot of fun with the new shops. But when I look over at your shop, it's sad and bare. To think it was full of life last All Hallows' Eve celebration." Last year she had a fun reading corner for children along with a costume contest. It was a magical time that I was afraid wasn't going to happen this year.

"June," Ophelia jumped up. The chair smacked down on the gazebo. "The wands. Did you say the wands had Colton's fingerprints on them?"

"Yes. They weren't real. They were fake children's wands." I stood up and stared at her.

"I had gotten wands for the window display for a magical book theme for the All Hallows' Eve celebration. Colton was in charge of hanging them from the ceiling at all different levels the day Patty was murdered. We were having an argument in the back of the shop about the display because he wanted me to do a princess and the frog theme and when we went back to the front of the shop, the wands were gone. I accused Colton of hiding them." She looked out to the garden.

Eloise's voice and another voice were chatting away. The clouds parted and the moon beamed on the two women like a spot light.

"Alise," Ophelia backed up, knocking into the table, sending my chair to the ground and all the stuff in my bag tumbling out. "What are you doing here?"

Chapter Twenty

"Oh, do you think I was honestly going to sit idly by as you let my son rot in jail for something he didn't do?" Alise swept up the steps and came nose-to-nose with Ophelia.

"Okay, now." I wedged myself between them, bending down to pick up the contents of my bag from the floor of the gazebo.

Ophelia bent down next to me.

"What is she doing here?" she whispered in my ear as she helped me pick up the items.

"I don't know." I held my purse open for her to put my things back in. "I didn't even know you were coming."

I stood up and tugged off my cloak. I was suddenly getting hot.

"Alise." I gave her a hug and turned her away from seeing Ophelia. "It's so good to see you. I can tell you've been using the lotion on your dark spots." I brought her hand up to view and was happy to see it'd been working just fine.

"I do love it. And when Eloise sent a message with the pigeons that the two of you were coming to see me, I sent a note back to Colton." Her brows cocked. "Only to receive a note late today that he's in jail for the murder of Patty Potter." She tilted her head to the side, past me and shot Ophelia a death stare.

"I didn't forsake him." Ophelia busted past me and charged at Alise. "You always thought it was me."

"No. I told you years ago when you were the flirty little school girl that if you broke my son's heart, you'd have hell to pay. Well," Alise's shoulders straightened. "Hell is here."

"Alise," Eloise drew her arms into the air. Thunder clattered overhead. "We will not have discord in my home."

Alise and Ophelia didn't move.

"I invited each of you here so June and I don't have to travel all around." Eloise raked her fingers at the edges of her short red hair. "We will have dark tea along with dark treats."

"I will not." Alise drew back.

"You know." Ophelia dropped her head.

"Only because I too am a Dark-Sider." Eloise drew a sobbing Ophelia in her arms and enclosed her in her green velvet cloak.

Alise's eyes held a dark reserve that I couldn't place.

"We are an integrated community thanks to June's vision when she moved here. She was almost taken down by a Dark-Sider but was adult and mature enough to understand that the spiritual community was a dying breed and we are better together than apart." Eloise's words were strangely veiled.

"Do you mean to tell me that Colton doesn't know you are a Dark-Sider? I mean, I just found out from you, but Colton?" I didn't understand why she wouldn't have told him. Then it struck me. "Because you are prejudiced." I pointed to Alise and addressed Ophelia again, "And you knew we were an integrated community so you opened your shop here."

My intuition told me I was right. Forget the healthy eating in case I was pregnant. I grabbed a June's Gem and took a big bite.

"And," I continued as the chocolaty treat soothed my soul. "Patty and Patch Potter are also Dark-Siders, hence the pumpkin farm and living on the edge of the development. He knew that you were a Dark-Sider. That's what the two of you were discussing in the woods the night he died."

"Yes," Ophelia stepped out of Eloise's safe haven. Her eyes clouded with haziness. "But I didn't kill him and neither did Colton."

"You're right about that. And that's the only thing you are right about." Alise's bitter voice cut right through the chill in the air.

I held my hand up for Alise to stop talking.

"Patty gave us a hard time after I started to date Colton. He knew that Colton's family had protested the Order of Elders convention when they were starting to vote on the integration of villages. I love Colton and Patty knew they wouldn't accept me in their lives if they knew. I had been talking Colton into moving away as soon as we graduated."

"You mean manipulated?" Alise asked in a fierce tone. Eloise put a gentle hand on Alise's arm.

"Go on," I encouraged Ophelia.

"Then upon graduation, we immediately left without telling anyone. Patty had threatened to tell the Lances and I got Colton out of there before Patty could tell him. Colton came here with me under false pretenses." Ophelia's voice cracked. "Patch and Patty came to the bookstore the other day to drop off the flyers for the pumpkin farm and that's when Patty found me. He'd given up looking for me, but since he felt I ruined his life because our parents had planned on us marrying, he told me he was going to tell Colton everything. That was when I told Colton it was over between us. He didn't understand why and I have to believe he figured it out the night he saw Patty at the pumpkin patch and lost his mind. Now Patty is dead and Colton is the number one suspect."

"You fled, leaving my son to rot." Alise pushed Eloise's hand off her arm. "When you are just as much a suspect as he is. The scorned ex-girlfriend's secret is about to be revealed."

"No I didn't. I knew I couldn't help find the real killer if both of us were in jail. June has been looking into things. The wands are fake. Someone stole them from the bookstore that day." She pleaded her case between the three of us.

"Do you have any way of knowing who was in the shop? Like a camera or something?" I asked wondering if she had security cameras, which was unlikely.

"June!" She grabbed me and kissed my cheeks. "You are a genius!" The biggest smile crossed her lips. "I have the entire camera section. Those books love to compete with each other on who has the best pixels and range. I bet they have something on that day."

"Then it looks like I'm going to have to do some investigating in there tomorrow." I felt like this might be the puzzle piece we need.

"But that doesn't solve this." Eloise gestured between Ophelia and Alise. "I'm just not understanding your prejudice when I'm a Dark-Sider along with several others in the community. Oscar is a Dark-Sider where June is a Good-Sider. There is no difference now. Colton and Ophelia love each other with every fiber in their hearts and souls—you should be happy that another woman loves your son as much, if not more than you do."

"I would never hurt him." Ophelia gulped. "But you don't have to forgive me. Once Colton finds out that I've been hiding this from him, he won't forgive me and it will be over forever. The least you can do is put our differences aside and help me get the person who has framed him."

"Colton knows." Alise's chin drew down to her chest.

"What?" Ophelia asked in shocked. "He knows?"

Mr. Prince Charming darted under the café table as if he was taking cover from an explosion that was about to take place.

"After you moved here, I went home and did a little investigative work myself because I knew it wasn't like him to up and move away from his beloved childhood village. I went back to the University and it was there that I met Patty Potter. He was all too happy to tell me about you and how you'd lied to my son. I came home and told Colton. At first he refused to believe me, then he went out there."

"You mean when he told me he was doing a wizard conference he was finding Patty?" Ophelia had told me about him going out of town and I had found it odd since Oscar hadn't gone, but Oscar didn't seem to be curious so I had let it go.

"Yes. He and Colton had gotten into a fight then. You wonder why I haven't been back to visit since you moved here and why I order everything through June instead of coming to visit and stock up—it is because Colton picked you over me." Alise's voice trailed off, a tear ran down her cheek. "He told me he didn't care if you never told him the truth. He knew your heart and he was going to be with you forever."

"June," Ophelia looked at me. "You have to sneak me into the jail. You said Oscar was in Locust Grove. I have to see Colton."

It didn't take long for me to agree and gather my things. Eloise and Alise weren't going to let us go alone. Eloise disappeared into her garden and came back with four Lightning Lights flowers. They reminded me of what mortals called the Buttercup only a light showed our way through the dark forest as we held the stem.

Mr. Prince Charming trotted off in his own direction.

"Can I ask you something about Darla and Dad?" I asked, carefully watching my step so as not to tumble over a fallen tree or branch. Eloise nodded. "How did it work as a mortal and spiritualist marriage?"

"Are you asking for knowledge or because you are trying to play matchmaker?" Eloise asked before we ducked to miss a bat soaring through the air.

"Both I guess." I stepped over a pile of dried leaves. "I think there is a true love connection like my parents that's brewing between two people in our new community and I'd like to encourage it."

Jo Ellen stayed on my mind. I would like her mom to be happy and the same with Gene. But I wanted Violet to be happy. But there was only one Patch Potter. Both women seemed to have an interest in him. I'd felt the electricity between Tish and Patch, which made me lean more toward a union between the two of them.

"First, Patch would have to come clean with Tish," Eloise let me know she'd already seen the future and I was talking about those two. "Tish would have to go through a ceremony where she gives up her mortal heritage and pledges a life to the spiritual community. That is not easy. Especially when there is a child involved and brought into the relationship, because Jo Ellen will never be a spiritualist unlike the possibility of a child between them, as you are." Eloise didn't make it sound easy. "But love overcomes many obstacles. The man is generally more reluctant to bring a woman into the mix if you understand what I mean. And most women aren't like Darla. She believed in the spiritual world before your father had started to court her."

Darla was definitely one of a kind. When I was a child I resented her odd ways, but now I wished I'd listened to her more and heeded her wisdom instead of tuning her out like most teenagers did with their parents.

"The best thing for you to do is to let them figure it out." As she spoke, I ran my hand down my bag and felt the pumpkin seed potion. I knew more than ever that Patch needed his own seeds to plant in his relationship.

So I wouldn't break any by-laws, I knew I could slip the potion into Tish's drink when I went back to check on the kitten. She'd be more than willing to accept the true Patch Potter.

Mr. Prince Charming darted in and out of the dark, batting at the fireflies that'd decided to join us.

"Ophelia," Colton slid down the bars of the cell when he saw us. He broke down into tears with his arms outstretched to her.

"I love you," Ophelia cried out and let him take her into his arms as she pressed up against the bars. "I'm so sorry. I wasn't going to leave you in here. I just wanted to find the killer."

"I knew you really loved me, but when I saw him my blood boiled and I knew that was the reason why you wanted us to end. I didn't tell anyone. I swear." He glanced over her shoulder and saw his mother.

"I. . ." Alise swallowed her pride and walked over to them. She bent down. "I want you to make me a proud mother and please get married after all of this."

My heart soared and my eyes welled with tears. Mr. Prince Charming stood up on his hind legs and swiped at my charm bracelet. The leaf charm dangled back and forth. There was change.

I rubbed my stomach when it gurgled and wondered if there was change going on inside me.

"It looks like we have a wedding to plan." Eloise clapped her hands together. Her lips pursed in a tight smile.

"Will you marry me?" Colton asked through tears.

"Yes," Ophelia and he sealed the deal with a kiss. Alise rubbed a hand on both of their heads before she curled Ophelia into a hug.

"I'm so sorry for my prejudice." She sobbed and held her soon-to-be daughter-in-law.

Mr. Prince Charming purred and dragged his tail along the bars of the jail before he looked at me.

Rowl.

"You don't have to stay here." I was sure that Mr. Prince Charming was telling me to let him out.

"June is right." Eloise grabbed the keys off of Oscar's desk. "The by-laws stated that if you are under investigation you can't leave Whispering Falls."

"I know, but when Ophelia left, I was safe from myself if I stayed in here." Colton stood up. "But I've got someone to live for and a wedding to plan. Let me out."

"You can have the honors." Eloise handed Alise the key and we watched as she turned the lock.

Colton ran out and whisked Ophelia into his arms, giving her a kiss that sent all of our hearts aflutter.

Chapter Twenty-One

There was something new in the air this morning. Maybe it had to do with magic in the air now that I'd put away the notion that Ophelia or Colton had anything to do with Patty's murder or the fact that they were back together like they should be. Or that I was going to play matchmaker today between Tish and Patch. But something tickled my insides.

Even though I wasn't going out of town to pay Alise a visit, I was still going to use Faith at the shop and take the opportunity to run into Locust Grove. I needed to run to the grocery store there and maybe stop by to say hi to Adeline. She was a friend of mine from way back and the owner of Piggly Wiggly.

Oscar wouldn't be back until this afternoon from there, so my schedule was wide open. I was also going to stop by Ever After Books and check out those books Ophelia said might've caught someone stealing the wands. If we could find that out, that would be our killer. My intuition told me I was right.

I would go there first, but I wanted to give her and Colton some time together. After what they'd gone through, they needed it.

Alise had gone to stay at Eloise's and I'd slept a little later than normal. Even Mr. Prince Charming was still curled up on Oscar's empty pillow. He purred as I dragged my hand over him a few times, giving him a good scratch under his chin before I got up and got ready.

The sun had even popped out over the village and burned off the early morning fog between Locust Grove and Whispering Falls. Mr. Prince Charming had curled up in the hot spot on the dashboard. The Green Machine hugged the curves of the old country road back to my hometown.

I scored a parking spot up in front of the Piggly Wiggly. It was probably still too early for a lot of the grocery shoppers. The smell of Wicked Good donuts rushed by me as the front doors of the grocery store parted and I walked in. It was so fun to see the display Faith had made in the front of the pastry section.

I glanced up to the ceiling and scanned down the front of the aisle, reading what was in each aisle. When I saw the feminine section, I headed that way. Slowly I walked down the shelves and tucked the nervous feeling inside of me away. I had to know and there it was. A pregnancy test.

"Goodness." There were so many different ones. Ovulating ones, double line ones, single line, boy or girl, and many more. I picked one up and read the back of it.

"If it's not a sight for sore eyes," Adeline called from the end of the aisle. "I wondered if you were ever going to come visit."

"Adeline." I was happy to see my sweet mortal friend. She had her sandy blond hair pulled up in a ponytail, her Piggly Wiggly green uniform shirt tucked in a pair of khaki's and that beaming, white smile.

We met in the middle of the aisle and embraced. She pulled away and grabbed my wrist, taking a look at the box.

"Oh my God!" She screamed. "You," she put her hand on my stomach, "can't be that far along. You are tiny."

"I don't know." I rattled the box in the air.

"That is wonderful." She wrapped her arm around me and squeezed before we started to walk to the front of the store. "I can't wait to see who he or she looks like most. I mean, Oscar," she fanned herself, "his eyes. Dreamy."

"I know." I gushed, feeling a tiny bit of excitement at the possibility. "Come by the shop and see me."

"I will. The seasonal rush swamps us." She smiled. "I keep up with you when Oscar comes in to get a salad from the salad bar for lunch. He said you're doing great." She gave me one last hug. "Let me know about the baby."

"There might not be a baby," I muttered after she scurried off.

I'd left the windows down to let the cool breeze in while I was in the grocery store, but Mr. Prince Charming was unfazed that I'd gone into the store. He was curled tight in a ball, still on the dashboard.

The day was actually turning out to be a nice sunny day. Not only would it be a good day to solve the murder of Patty Potter, it'd be a good day to find out if I was going to be a mom.

After I parked the Green Machine at the cottage, I headed down the hill toward Blue Moon Gallery. I wanted to get a look at the photos Faith had taken and I hoped Cherry had hung them up like Perry said she was going to.

"What do I owe the pleasure?" Cherry greeted me and Mr. Prince Charming when we walked through the gallery door.

"Faith Mortimer's photos." It was really great to see Faith's photos coming to life. "My friend Colton Lance is a suspect in Patty Potter's murder and I don't think he did it, so I'm wanting to check out Faith's photos to see if there was anything suspicious."

"Oh, June," she sucked in a deep breath. She had on a long, flowing silk kimono with paint brushes embroidered all over it. At the end of the paint brushes, there were little bursts of fireworks. "You have no idea. I'm so glad you are here."

Her words didn't have a happy-to-see-you tone. It was more of an I'm not sure what to do.

"The best photo Faith took is the pumpkin farm. There is nothing unusual in it, but it sends my gift into a spiral." She gestured for me to follow her. She talked over her shoulder as we walked, "I hesitate to put it out because my gift tells me something is wrong with this photo. Since you are telling me about the possibility that she has captured something, you might be right and that is why I'm questioning the picture."

Mr. Prince Charming didn't follow us. He sat under a photo that was hanging from the ceiling.

She stopped at the glass staircase and dragged out a large frame covered in brown paper.

"I went ahead and sent it off to be framed and I've yet to look at it." She ripped the paper off. She shuddered and looked away.

I bent down and looked at it. Faith had really captured the essence of the happiness shown on all of our faces. The pumpkins were bright orange even in the dark. The twinkle lights strung all over the pumpkin farm added to the charm. In the photo she'd captured Jo Ellen eating the candy apple, Oscar hanging out with Hazel as they talked to a dark-haired man, Petunia sitting on a pumpkin petting a field mouse that was perched on her finger, Izzy sitting next to her enjoying a cup of hot cider, the Karima twins eating their own bag of kettle corn, and more of the new citizens I didn't know.

I looked back at Oscar. The dark-haired man looked familiar.

"I'll be right back." I stood up and walked over to Mr. Prince Charming. "This one?" I asked. His tail pointed up to the photo.

It was another pumpkin farm photo that Faith had taken during the day. Next to the shed where I'd heard

Patch and Patty fighting stood Patch, Tish, and that dark-haired man.

"Do you have a magnifying glass?" I asked Cherry.

"I do." She trotted up the glass steps to where her office was and came right back down. "Here you go."

I held the magnifying glass up to the spot I questioned on the photo. All three of their faces didn't seem very happy. The faces weren't very clear, but he had a prominent silhouette with a large nose. The dark-haired man had a finger pointing at Patch.

I took the magnifying glass back over to the photo and looked at the same dark-haired man in the photo. It was a little further away and Faith had used some sort of filter on the camera, but the profile sure did look the same.

"You are the best." I handed Cherry the magnifying glass before Mr. Prince Charming and I left. I pulled my phone out of my bag and called Oscar. "Hi honey," I left a message when he didn't answer. "I wanted to let you know I might have a lead. Call me."

The street was filled with visitors and the crisp air felt like the All Hallows' Eve celebration. It was going to be tomorrow night with or without the murder solved. The brochures were in all of the shop windows along with their displays. The costume contest was going to be the cutest. It reminded me that I'd forgotten to get candy.

I called Oscar back and asked him to grab some candy for Wicked Good and A Charming Cure for the trick-or-treat part of the celebration. It was so good to see Ever After Books decorated. It wasn't open yet, but I knocked on the display window and peeked in covering my eyes with my hands. When Colton saw me, he walked over to the door to let me in.

Mr. Prince Charming scooted on down to Glorybee Pet Shop. He'd probably had enough human interaction for one day.

The bookstore was so magical. The animals brayed, mooed, chirped, and clucked when I walked past the animal reference section. The crying and oohing baby noises crept down the baby aisle. I rubbed my stomach wondering if I was going to have to get one of those books tomorrow. The voices of scholars yelled over each other as I passed by that aisle. The books came to life. The bird books were flying throughout the store and would land anywhere.

"It's so good to see you two." I couldn't stop the smile.

"We are so happy." Ophelia looked at Colton. He was putting the finishing touches on the fairy tale window. "I let him win." She winked.

"The window looks great." I looked around for the camera and photo aisle. "I wanted to get a look at the books."

"Yeah. I waited until you got here to open. I figured they'd show off for you. Sometimes books can be crabby." She came from behind the counter and I followed her to the back corner of the shop.

It was fascinating to watch Ophelia Biblio do her thing. She closed her eyes and dragged her finger along the spines of the books that were on the shelves. The sounds of cameras clicking erupted as she got closer. She stopped at a book with a thick green spine. Her finger ran up the spine and she used her fingernail to pluck it off the shelf. The book tumbled down, bounced on its spine a couple of times before it fell open to a page.

With her eyes still closed, Ophelia bent down and pointed to the page. When she slowly stood up, the book flashed photos of the shop with Colton in the back holding a couple of the fake wands in the air.

I stepped over to get a closer look. I searched the photos as the book clicked them through as if it were an air photo album. There had to be some sort of clue in there and it would be great if there were something to tie someone from Faith's photos to someone in the store.

"There!" I pointed in the air.

Ophelia opened her eyes and snapped the photo out of thin air and made it physical. She handed it to me.

I held it up and she looked over my shoulder to look at it.

"I don't see anything." She squinted.

"There you and Colton are next to the counter." I pointed to them. Their heads were together.

"That's when we were fighting." Sadness hung on the edge of her words.

"Don't worry about that." I used my open hand to rub her back. "See the dark-haired guy at the front of the shop?"

She dipped her head forward to get a better look.

"You've got good eyes." She squinted. "I see the silhouette."

"That same guy is in some of Faith's photos." I left out all the details. "I don't know who he is but I can place him here. And it sure does look like a wand in his hand."

"You are an angel!" She squealed. "Colton! I think June knows who killed Patty."

"Whoa." I stopped her from getting her hopes up. "I don't know him but I plan on finding out." I shook the photo. "Can I take this with me?"

"Absolutely." Her eyes grew. "Go! Figure this out so we can open and enjoy All Hallows' Eve."

The excitement in her voice put a little giddy-up in my step. I was more determined than ever to get to the bottom of this. And the only way to do that was to visit Patch and ask him who this man was.

The day was getting away from me so I darted up behind the police station and headed straight to the pumpkin farm instead of grabbing the Green Machine. Sometimes by foot was quicker than by wheels.

I tried to call Oscar again, but it went straight to voicemail. Maybe he was listening to his messages and was going to call me back. I left another message to call me because I felt like there was a connection between clues. Patch was in one of the photos talking to the man so I knew he'd be able to at least identify him. My phone beeped to let me know it was dying.

The pumpkin farm was closed and I had to straddle a few pumpkins on my way through it, careful not to trip over the thick vines that seemed to make a thorny maze for me. No wonder Mr. Prince Charming didn't want to come.

Across the field I heard someone calling my name. Jo Ellen was in her backyard, her arms waving to me over her head. When I waved back, she bent down and picked up the white kitten, dangling her in the air to show me.

I made my way over to her house. I might as well check on her and the kitten like I had promised Petunia.

"How do you like Snow White?" she asked.

"Perfect name." I took Snow White from her and rubbed my hands down her fur. I looked up at the house. "Where's your mom?"

"She's inside with my dad. Fighting." She rolled her eyes. "They needed parent time. That means they are arguing. My dad actually took my side for once."

"Oh yeah." I was curious what that meant. If I was about to become a parent, I needed all the ammunition on how these little people's minds worked.

"Yeah. He had me a fun wizard costume with little wands and all. But she wanted me to be a princess because my wands are missing." Her lips turned down. "Daddy brought me new ones today, but Mommy was so mad."

I glanced up at the house. My gut tugged. Her wands went missing? Tish appeared at the back glass door, a man with dark hair next to her.

"Look at this ugly doll he gave me. I don't even like dolls," disappointment rang in her voice.

Turn to the side, my head begged as the knot in my throat nearly stopped my breathing. I didn't have the effort to look at Jo's doll.

"Hi, June!" Tish yelled after she opened the door. "Jo Ellen Broussert, come say 'bye to your daddy."

It took everything I had in my body to wave back and put a smile on my face. Not only did I have physical evidence that Broussert was at the bookstore and the pumpkin farm, he wasn't on vacation like Oscar had thought. Plus he had a motive to kill Patch from what Hazel said.

I watched as the dark-haired man wrapped Jo in his arms and slid my eyes down to the doll. I reached down and picked up a homemade voodoo doll.

Chapter Twenty-Two

I stumbled across the yard trying to make my way to Patch's house. If I could make it past Hazel's yard, I knew Patch would be a safe haven. My theory of Broussert killing Patty believing he was Patch made more sense than ever. Not only did I have the photo evidence, I had the voodoo doll that looked almost identical to the one found at the crime scene.

"Oscar, where are you?" I stopped once I made it over to Hazel's yard and out of sight of Tish's back door. I held the voodoo doll up to my face. "I know who killed Patty."

I took my phone down from my ear and noticed it'd died. I threw it in my bag.

"June? Honey, you okay?" Hazel suddenly stood up from her rose garden. She was rubbing her hand on her hip.

"I'm fine." I waved the voodoo doll in the air before I stuck it in my bag. I tugged my wrist when my charm bracelet caught.

"Let me help you." She waddled over and looked at the bracelet. "Oh, honey. My eyes can't help you."

"It's okay." I got myself free. I pulled away and started toward Patch's.

"Where are you going in such a hurry?" she asked. "Come in for some tea. You look like you could use something. You are looking a little peaked."

"No thank you." I shook my head.

"June, if you are pregnant, you need to keep hydrated." And she had to go there.

I could wait for Oscar to call me back and then go over to Patch's. As long as I wasn't with Tish.

"Okay. I could use a refresher." It was nice to see that I pleased Hazel.

We walked into her house and she insisted I sit on the couch and rest while she got my tea.

I was so nervous I wasn't able to sit still. I walked around the family room, taking a look outside over the pumpkin farm.

"Have you seen Patch?" I asked.

"Last time I saw him, he was going to the farm to meet Broussert." Her words were like knives to my ears.

"Oh no." I gasped, wondering if Broussert was going to take that opportunity to finish the job he botched. I dragged my eyes across the wall to look at her in the kitchen and the photo of her and her grandson and son caught my eyes.

"Oh no, what?" she asked.

An uneasiness spiced with irritation coiled deep in my bones as my eyes focused on the dark-haired man that had the exact same nose as the man in all the photos. I composed myself and walked into the kitchen. Hazel smiled at me as she stirred the iced tea in the glass.

"I'm not thirsty. I'm going to be going. I'm going to be late to meet Oscar." I gave her a hug and noticed the insect killer in the white bottle sitting on the kitchen windowsill. There was a small white trail from the window to the glass.

"I really think you need to drink for the baby." She pulled back and glanced in the direction of the bug killer.

Suddenly I felt dizzy as I read the banner across the bug killer. *Boric Acid.*

"Well, fiddlesticks." Hazel took a step back. "I was afraid of this. When I saw you with my cute little doll I had made, I figured you weren't stupid. And now this." She waddled over and picked up the bug killer. "Broussert promised my son the farm job. He promised me Patch's property. I'm an old lady and just want to spend my last days with my grandson, son and my roses. I have bad eyes." She tapped her eye. "So when I offered Patch an iced tea with a little of the boric acid, I had no idea it was his brother until you mentioned it. I honestly thought I didn't give him enough. After all, he was so tired from the events of the night when I popped over there to see him after everyone left."

"It's okay. I understand." I refused to take the glass as she held it up to me.

"Since you understand, then you should have no problem drinking this." She held it up to my face.

"No thank you. I'm going to leave." I moved around her and headed to the front door.

"Edwin, she's trying to leave," she said as I made my way down the hall. I had to get out of there.

"Hi," the dark-haired man stood between me and the door. "I'm going to have to ask you to stay for a beverage." His head tilted side-to-side as if he was joking around with me.

"Oh, I can't, but thank you." I pushed my hand around him to grab the handle of the door.

"Well, it's not up to you." He pulled out a gun and stuck it in my gut.

"I'm pregnant." The words tumbled out of my mouth.

"Not for long." He shoved the gun deeper in my stomach, forcing me to take a step back.

The knock at the door threw us all for a loop.

"Oscar is here." I saw him from the window. He was looking over toward Patch's house.

"Don't say a word or I kill you both," he said in a deep, low voice that told me he meant business.

Edwin put his finger up to his mouth to tell me to hush and pointed the gun to the other room so I was out of sight when he opened the door. On my way down the hall, I set my bag in view of the door hoping Oscar was observant enough to see it.

Hazel sat in her chair sipping on her cup of tea with a smile on her face and a shotgun at her feet. As sweet as pie, but the devil inside.

"You know that Patch fellow is crazy. I overheard him saying something to Tish about having some kind of psychic power." Hazel rolled her eyes. "The world is much better off without that quack. He'll be joining you and his brother soon enough."

Even though I should be thinking how I could get out of there alive, I was happy to hear that Patch was opening up to Tish and maybe they had a shot of a mortal-spiritualist relationship, even if she was Broussert's ex-wife and Jo Ellen was his daughter.

Edwin walked back into the kitchen. "Got rid of him. He said he'd gotten your message and the nosy neighbor kid told him you walked over here with her dolly. I told him I was visiting my sweet mom and we hadn't seen you." His evil grin curled up on his lips like a snake.

He walked back in the family room and stood in front of the back door, facing me and holding the glass of poison. "Now you must kill yourself, right Mom?"

"Right, boy. Then you can go over to the farm and get rid of that crazy Patch Potter so you can move in next door and take over his job like Broussert had promised you in the first place." They both stared at me.

In a flash, the glass of the back door shattered as Oscar bolted through, sending shards of glass everywhere, one sticking right in Hazel's hand that was holding the shotgun and one in the chest of Edwin.

The last thing I remember before it went black was Edwin falling right on top of me and the glass of poison dripping down my leg.

Chapter Twenty-Three

"Good morning." I'd know those lips anywhere. I smiled underneath the kiss and let Oscar's sweet voice drift in my ears. "You've been asleep long enough."

"Have I?" I questioned. My brain turned on. I sat straight up. I glanced around the room. "What happened?"

"Smart move on the bag." He ran his hand down the back on my head before he curled me into his arms. "You scared me. I was at the farm waiting for Broussert to come so I could question him about his wife. Patch was there and he told me that Broussert was going to be late because he was at his ex-wife's house. He went on, telling me how Broussert said something strange was going on in the agri-hood because the wizard outfit he bought his daughter went missing so I naturally thought you were right about Broussert so I zoomed over to the bookstore because you mentioned something about photos and I'd heard from Colton that you were there earlier when he called to let me know he'd left the jail." His heart pounded beneath his chest. I was never so glad to hear his beating heart. "Then Ophelia told me about the dark-haired man and again, I thought of Broussert. I raced back to the agri-hood and over to Tish's house where Broussert was still there and I had a few words with them. I found out that it's Tish who wants the Crazy Crafty Chick because apparently she understands what it means to marry a spiritualist."

I pulled back.

"She told you that in front of Broussert?" I asked.

"No, she pulled me aside and told me that she and Patch were in love and she wanted to marry him. He did what we are supposed to do in those situations, gave her a memory spell about the conversation, if the spell erases the conversation from the recipient's mind, then true love doesn't prevail. If the recipient remembers the conversation, a spell can't be put against them because love prevailed."

"So that's what happened between Darla and Dad," I let out a heavy sigh and nuzzled back up against Oscar.

"After I saw Edwin at the door with dark hair and your bag on the ground, plus Mr. Prince Charming sitting on the front porch, I knew you were in there."

I looked over at Mr. Prince Charming curled up at the edge of the bed. He might be ornery at times, but he did his job.

"I called Colton for backup and I saw you in there on the couch and I had to crash through. Both confessed to the murder. Edwin had planned on pinning it on Broussert—he knew Broussert bought his daughter the wizard outfit so he stole the wands from Ever After Books to tie the murder to Broussert. The voodoo doll was Hazel's idea because she said he was a freak physic or something like that when Colton was hauling her off."

"And of course I blacked out." I laughed.

"Big Edwin landing on you didn't help, but he only has a few scratches from the glass stabbing him." He kissed the top of my head. "I'm not sure I'm going to let you help me anymore. You stick to the potion making and being the sweet-natured little witch."

"We will see." I pulled away and stood up. I needed to go to the bathroom. The pregnancy test said first thing in the morning. "I'll be right back."

I paddled down the hallway and found my purse on the counter. I took out the test and headed to the bathroom.

After a few minutes I looked at it.

Negative. I held it for a few seconds, taking in my feelings and what exactly that meant.

"June, are you coming to back to bed?" Oscar asked. "We have a few minutes before we have to get up for the All Hallows' Eve celebration.

"Yeah," I called back and buried the pregnancy test in the bathroom garbage can before I headed into the bedroom where I found Oscar with a wry grin on his face. "What are you up to?"

"Come here and find out." He reached for me and curled me into his warm, safe arms. "So are you?"

"Am I what?" I looked up at him. The look of love in his big blue eyes spread to his lips.

"Are you pregnant?" he asked.

"No." I lowered my eyes. "How did you know?"

"I ran into Adeline at the Piggly Wiggly when I was getting the candy and she asked me if congratulations were in order." He grinned.

"Are you upset?" I asked.

"Are you?"

"No." I wasn't upset. But one thing the idea of being pregnant did give me was certainty that one day I did hope to become a mom. Just not today.

"I think we could use more practice. Lots more practice." Oscar teased before he clicked off the bedside table light and covered Madame Torres with a pillow.

"Thank you," Madame Torres muffled with a grateful voice. And Mr. Prince Charming ran out of the room.

Chapter Twenty-Four

Excitement was in the air and there was no denying that All Hallows' Eve had come. Every shop owner in Whispering Falls had their doors open, their windows decorated, and a bowl full of candy waiting for all the children to come and partake in the ceremonies.

"Hi, June!" Jo Ellen ran inside A Charming Cure wearing her costume.

"Ms. Heal." Tish reminded her.

"June is fine." I smiled and noticed Jo Ellen was now a cowgirl. "Another change in costume?" I asked.

"Yes" Jo bounced on the toes of her tiny pink cowboy boots. She held out her Halloween basket in the shape of a horse's saddle. "I couldn't leave Miss Princess Charming at home."

"Miss Princess Charming?" I looked into the basket. The little white kitten was curled up on the bottom. "I thought you named her Snow White?"

"I had to name her after Mr. Prince Charming." She swayed back and forth.

Mr. Prince Charming must've heard his name. He darted out from underneath the table where he'd been all day since I'd put a small bowtie cat collar on him.

"Oh, Mommy! Look." Jo giggled. "He has on a costume. Can we get Miss Princess Charming a costume?"

"Thanks, June." Tish glared at me and I laughed. "Maybe next year."

Jo took it better than I thought and she sat down on the floor of the shop to pet my ornery cat.

"Can I get you an apple cider?" I asked, walking over to counter.

"You know, I'd love some." She had bent down and patted Mr. Prince Charming. She looked up at me. "That sounds really good."

The shop was empty because I'd left Faith to hand out the candy for the tourists next to the gate so the parents didn't have to police their children inside the shop.

"I hear that you and Patch have made a special bond." I knew that he'd been talking to her about our special village secret and had yet to hear her response. I walked over and grabbed the potion I'd created a few days ago, not really sure why I'd created it, but my intuition told me that Tish needed a little of it.

Not necessarily to fall in love with Patch, but to be open to the idea.

"I mean, you don't have to tell me." I slipped a couple of drops in her cider and stirred it with a cinnamon stick that I'd gotten from Happy Herb. It added the extra flavor that gave the cider a little kick. "Just sometimes we girls need to stick together." I held the cup out for her when she stood up.

"Some of us girls aren't cut from the same cloth." She blew on her cider and her eyes hooded as her brows lifted to mine. "I have Jo Ellen to think about."

"Do you see these two people?" I walked over to the framed photo of my parents. "They are my parents. My father was a police officer here like Oscar and my mother tried to create homeopathic cures. I was a little girl when my father died. Younger than Jo Ellen. My mother had to move away from Whispering Falls into Locust Grove." I knew the little bit of back story into my history told Tish that my mother was like her. "It wasn't until my mother died and I was an adult did I find out who I really was along with my heritage." I rubbed my finger down the glass on the frame. "My mother loved it here. She owned this very shop years before I took it over. And my cottage on the hill," I gestured behind me, "was their home."

"I'd talked to Broussert about having a shop here." She left Jo's side and walked over to me. "Because I would love to have something here. But according to Patch, and from what he's told me about your lives, I don't think I could do that."

I'd recalled how I'd heard Broussert had wanted to buy Crazy Crafty Chick, but this wasn't the time to discuss that.

"You never know until you try." I shrugged and looked over her shoulder when the bell above the entrance rang when the door opened.

"Patch!" Jo jumped up from the floor and ran over into his arms. "Look."

He looked down into the basket and saw the kitten.

"Miss Princess Charming looks very comfortable, squirt." He picked her up and held her in his arms. His eye drifted across the shop and melted on Tish's face.

She caught a breath as though it'd suddenly struck her or my potion just kicked in.

"Hi Patch." Her voice was soft and sincere. "I've. . .I've been thinking."

"Please excuse me for a minute." I didn't want to impose on a private moment between them, even though I might've helped it along a tiny bit. Deep in my heart, I knew they were meant to be together with or without my potion.

Patch smiled as I walked out the door and stood on the porch.

Faith was surrounded by all the little kids in so many different costumes. Oscar ran across the street from the police station.

"Big turn out this year." He kissed me. I curled an arm around his waist and clasped my hands together. "Look at all those cute kids."

"I know." I sucked in a deep breath, letting the crisp air sink into my lungs and drip into my soul. "One of these days we will have a little one running around for candy."

"Oh yeah." Oscar smiled. There was a twinkle in his eyes.

"Yeah." I had determined that I did want to have children and bring more little Parks into the spiritual world. "Just not right now."

Meow. Mr. Prince Charming appeared next to me and did figure eights around my ankles.

"He's enough for now." I bent down and picked him up. He purred in my arms and even let Oscar pet him.

"Hi, June!" KJ called from the front of his shop. He was dressed in his real Native American dress. It was perfect for the festivities.

"Hi!" I waved. My mouth dropped when I saw him put his hand on Violet's back. She looked at me and grinned ear-to-ear.

"Do you still want to take me and Gene to visit the school?" Violet asked.

"Yes. I'd love to." I was happy knowing she'd taken my advice.

"I think the outfit is working for him." Oscar joked as we watched Violet and KJ hug, letting the village know they were a couple.

"She loves more than the outfit." I looked back at Faith.

"There's just something special about All Hallows' Eve." Faith glanced over at Violet and KJ, and then back at Patch, Tish, and Jo Ellen standing behind us.

"'Bye Mr. Prince Charming." Jo skipped past us with Patch and Tish following closely behind her, holding hands.

"'Bye," I said.

"Thank you." Tish mouthed when she walked past.

I looked down the sidewalk at all the children in their costumes and their parents standing near them. All of the spiritualists were dressed with a nod to some characteristic of their real gift.

Chandra had her turban on and a sign around her neck that said *Palm Reader*. Petunia was dressed as herself with a bird sitting on her shoulder. Colton and Ophelia were giving out candy on the steps of Ever After Books, both dressed in Harry Potter robes. Izzy was on the steps of Mystic Lights, dressed as a crystal ball reader. Gerald was too busy serving food, dressed as himself. Of course the line to get a bakery treat from Wicked Good was long and Raven was dressed as a chef. Chandler was outside and dressed in a candle outfit with a fake flame hat. He was talking to Bella and Eloise.

Everyone was back to normal in Whispering Falls. The light breeze blew across my nose, lifting my spirits even more. Faith was right. There was something special and magical about All Hallows' Eve.

"This is the best turn out yet," Oscar said.

"Yes it is." I took another look around.

"Shall we go check out all the shops?" he asked, putting his elbow out for me to take.

"I'd love to." I took a deep breath and my soul twanged.

Whispering Falls was growing and I couldn't help but feel that something was lurking. . .something mysterious.

Find out where it all began!
Chapter One of A CHARMING CRIME

"I know, I know." I waved my hands in front of me trying to stop anything that was about to come out of Oscar Park's mouth, but I knew it was useless.

He slammed the door of his patrol car, took his hat off, and then waved it toward my shed. . .my burning shed. "You know what?"

Truth be told, I didn't know much, but I did know how to handle Oscar Park. Especially when it came to personal matters. "I know I went a bit too far this time, but I really need to figure out this new cure."

Oscar grew up across the street, raised by his uncle, Police Chief Jordan Parks. Like me, well sort of like me, Oscar's parents got killed in a car accident while my dad was shot in the line of duty.

"A bit?" Oscar shook his head and pointed to the flames shooting up in the air. "Unless you want the new cure to blow someone up, I think you were using the wrong ingredients."

"Now, Oscar." I shuffled out of the way of the zipping fire truck, and took a bite of the Ding Dong in my hand that I had grabbed on the way out of the shed when I knew it was going to combust. "Was it necessary to call in all of Locust Grove's finest?"

"Yes, June Heal." Oscar wasn't the ten-year-old boy who created havoc with me in that very shed while experimenting with my mom Darla's homeopathic cures. Though his crystal blue eyes were sincere, I knew he meant business. "But you've done it this time. It's a total loss."

I held the uneaten round end of the Ding Dong up to him and he took a bite. A big bite. I grumbled under my breath. He knew Ding Dongs are my go-to comfort food.

Old Mac McGurtle came running through the herb garden I had planted after Darla died, screaming, "I told you she was going to set this whole town on fire if she kept mixing those chemicals."

Mr. McGurtle was always spreading gossip since Darla died about how I had turned A Dose of Darla, my homeopathic cure shop, into a fire hazard by putting all sorts of crazy concoctions together.

"Settle down, Mr. McGurtle." Jordan Parks snuck up behind us. "Thank you for calling us, and helping Ms. Heal save her business."

"Hhmph." Mr. McGurtle threw his hands in the air and mumbled something under his breath.

"He's the one who called?" I huffed, my bangs flew out of my eyes, and I crossed my arms. "He needs to mind his own business. And stop walking through my herb garden!"

For a moment Mr. McGurtle and I stared at each other until Jordan stepped between us.

The shed looked like it was going to be a total loss this time. All the other twenty times I set it afire I was able to save it. Luckily, I only used the shed to create new homeopathic cures using Darla's old remedies. I kept the main ingredients in the basement of our old house. . .my house now.

"I think you did it this time," Jordan warned, half serious. He walked away shaking his head. He stopped briefly to talk to one of the guys from the fire department.

"Not only have you done it this time, you've really pissed off a lot of your neighbors." Oscar put his hat back on his head, and looked around at the neighbors gathering on the other side of the fence in my front yard. "They think you are as crazy as Darla was."

Darla Heal, my mother, was the creator of A Dose of Darla, homeopathic cures. And everyone called her Darla, even me, because she didn't like to be referred to as Ms. Heal, Mrs. Heal or even Mom.

"Well, the old saying is right then." I snarled, studying every face gawking at me. They were just being nosy like always.

"And what old saying it that?" Oscar asked.

"The apple," I pointed to myself, "doesn't fall too far from the tree."

Oscar's face split into a wide grin. "And we sure did have some fun times in there. But you've got to admit you've outgrown this place and selling your cures at the flea market."

I wish I had another Ding Dong. I listened to what he had to say. He was right. The retail space for A Dose of Darla had started in the shed until Darla moved it to a booth at the local flea market. She had all sorts of people coming to get her homeopathic cures. And she had been good at it.

I spent most of my teenage years working Darla's booth at the flea market with Oscar right next to me, and hated every moment of it. I always swore I'd never take over Darla's business. As they say, never say never. When Darla died from an apparent heart attack, I did the only thing I could to take care of myself. I took over A Dose of Darla and began to experiment.

Most of the remedies needed to be updated, and since I had always been good in chemistry, I knew I could make them better. Making them better meant doing a lot of combinations of different things and not getting them to explode. Unfortunately, today was not a good mix of ingredients.

"You know I don't want to live in the country with all those scary noises." I knew what Oscar was hinting at.

For weeks, he'd been begging me to get rid of this old house and move to a farm where I could make a real lab, so I could create my remedies the right way. Not in a shed.

"Not in the country." He leaned in a little closer, and said words tentatively as if testing the idea, "I stumbled upon a little village about thirty minutes from here when I went to check out a job opening. I have a good feeling about it. But keep it on the down low."

I drew back to take in his expression. "You can't leave the police department here." I was pretty good at reading him all these years, almost psychic, but the sun cast a shadow on his face, making it hard for me to see if he was serious.

"Shhh." He held his finger up to his lips. "I said down low, not out loud. I will be by tonight to tell you about it. And it really is something you need to consider."

He definitely had my wheels turning as I stood in a puddle of water created by the fire department in their efforts to save the shed, only their efforts had been a waste. Jordan informed me that the fire chief told him the shed was a total loss. As if I needed to be told. All that was left was the cement foundation. Who knew that Thea Sinensis mixed with Camellia was so flammable? I did now. Thank God, because the cure I had been making had been for me. I could really see Mr. McGurtle's face if I had been blow up.

I swear I saw Mr. McGurtle smiling all the way from his front yard.

"Excuse me! Excuse me!" a woman yelled from the other side of the fence. She waved when she caught my eye. "Yes, you!" She pointed at me.

I was glad to see everyone but she had left. The show was finally over and I could get back to work. . . except I couldn't. Not without the shed.

The lady was someone I didn't recognize. The floral A-line skirt was throwing me off a bit, but the black, lace-up booties were definitely awesome. The closer I got, the more she reminded me of a younger version of Meryl Streep, the blond hair was long and wavy like Meryl's. Even her nose was small and pointed, only she had hazel eyes and sweeping lashes.

"Are you Darla from A Dose of Darla?" She pointed her lace gloved fingers toward my home.

"I'm Darla's daughter, June Heal." I put my hand out, but she didn't take it, so I pretended to rub them together. "Darla passed away a few years ago. Are you a friend?"

It wouldn't have been unusual for someone out of the blue to show up and visit with Darla. She had friends from all over. Darla was sort of a gypsy type. She believed in free spirit, holistic living, and open imagination. Darla taught me to be kind to everyone and everything.

"No." She scrunched her nose. "Did you take over the business?"

"I did." Something in my gut made me wearily suspicious of her.

"You sell something I might be interested in." She lowered her thick dark lashes, and stared at me.

"I, um, sell homeopathic remedies," I muttered uneasily.

Out of the corner of my eye, I could see Mr. McGurtle making his way back across the yard, as fast as his short legs could carry him. Through the herb garden. . .again.

"I was interested in selling them in my store." She pulled a business card out of the top of her glove. "Please come pay me a visit if you are interested. Good day."

I took the card from her fingers and we held a gaze for just a moment. Her eyes wandered over my shoulder. I turned around to find Mr. McGurtle giving her the wonky eye, which was his signature "don't mess with me" look.

When I turned back around, the strange woman was already in her car, pulling away from the curb.

"Do you need something, Mr. McGurtle?" I sighed walking past him toward the house.

Meow, Mr. Prince Charming sat on the top wooden porch step, dragging his tail back and forth. He batted at the cicada darting in the air.

The bottom of his tail was always black from all the wagging he did. It amazed me how, otherwise, he was always pristinely white. I'd assume keeping clean would be difficult for most outdoor cats. But Mr. Prince Charming was not like any other cat I'd ever come across.

"I promised Darla I'd keep a close eye on you," Mr. McGurtle said, stomping after me.

Rolling my eyes, I made it up on the porch before he yelled, "I think you are causing more trouble in your adult life than when you were a kid."

For a moment I stood still, trying to think of an answer while Mr. Prince Charming did figure eights around my ankles, but decided to bite my tongue. It was easier not to argue with Mr. McGurtle.

"Oh, Mr. Prince Charming, must you?" I bent down and flicked the dead cicada into the grass next to the steps with all the other dead ones he had killed. I swear he's on a mission to whack every cicada in Locust Grove. If the cat only knew the town was named after the nasty bugs—he'd be in heaven.

I flung the screen door open, and Mr. Prince Charming ran into the house before me. I closed the door behind me.

This was generally how Mr. McGurtle and I ended all of our conversations.

About the Author

For years, *USA Today* bestselling author Tonya Kappes has been self-publishing her numerous mystery and romance titles with unprecedented success. She is famous not only for her hilarious plotlines and quirky characters, but her tremendous marketing efforts that have earned her thousands of followers and a devoted street team of fans. Be sure to check out Tonya's website for upcoming events and news and to sign up for her newsletter! Tonyakappes.com

Also by Tonya Kappes

Olivia Davis Paranormal Mystery Series
SPLITSVILLE.COM
COLOR ME LOVE (novella)
COLOR ME A CRIME

Magical Cures Mystery Series
A CHARMING CRIME
A CHARMING CURE
A CHARMING POTION (novella)
A CHARMING WISH
A CHARMING SPELL
A CHARMING MAGIC
A CHARMING SECRET
A CHARMING CHRISTMAS (novella)
A CHARMING FATALITY
A CHARMING GHOST
A CHARMING HEX
A CHARMING VOODOO

Spies and Spells Series
Spies and Spells
Betting Off Dead
Get Witch or Die Trying (available for presale)

Grandberry Falls Series
THE LADYBUG JINX
HAPPY NEW LIFE
A SUPERSTITIOUS CHRISTMAS (novella)
NEVER TELL YOUR DREAMS

A Laurel London Mystery Series

CHECKERED CRIME
CHECKERED PAST
CHECKERED THIEF

A Divorced Diva Beading Mystery Series
A BREAD OF DOUBT SHORT STORY
STRUNG OUT TO DIE
CRIMPED TO DEATH

Bluegrass Romance Series
GROOMING MR. RIGHT
TAMING MR. RIGHT

Women's Fiction
CARPE BREAD 'EM

Young Adult
TAG YOU'RE IT

A Ghostly Southern Mystery Series
A GHOSTLY UNDERTAKING
A GHOSTLY GRAVE
A GHOSTLY DEMISE
A GHOSTLY MURDER
A GHOSTLY REUNION (available for presale)
A GHOSTLY MORTALITY (available for presale)

Copyright

Made in the USA
Middletown, DE
01 September 2018